NURSE IN CHARGE

When Amanda Wright arrived at Croxton Hall Nursing Home she left behind in London a phase of her life which had ended with the death of her mother. She met Doctor Richard Ormond, whose father, Charles, owned the Hall and lived on the adjoining farm. Richard was an intensely hard-working young man, and Amanda found herself in a position to help him solve a serious problem. But that was only one of a number of problems which arose to test her to the limit, and she tried to rise to the challenge with courage and determination.

NURSE IN CHARGE

Nurse In Charge

by

Lorna Page

Dales Large Print Books
Long Preston, North Yorkshire,
BD23 4ND, England.

British Library Cataloguing in Publication Data.

Page, Lorna
    Nurse in charge.

      A catalogue record of this book is
      available from the British Library

      ISBN   1-84262-067-3 pbk

First published in Great Britain by Robert Hale Ltd., 1979

Copyright © Lorna Page 1979

Cover illustration © McKenzie by arrangement with
P.W.A. International Ltd.

The moral right of the author has been asserted

Published in Large Print 2001 by arrangement with
Robert Hale Limited

Dales Large Print is an imprint of Library Magna Books Ltd.

Printed and bound in Great Britain by
T.J. (International) Ltd., Cornwall, PL28 8RW

ONE

Amanda Wright had fallen in love with Croxton Hall the first time she had seen it, when she had applied for the position of Nursing Sister there a month earlier. Now, leaning forward in the taxi which brought her out from the near-by town of Frampton, she studied the large greystone building anew and could not fault its Georgian appearance. The April sun was bright and warm, the sky a cloudless blue, and the rural setting for the house was fresh and green. The taxi turned off the road and followed a gravelled drive between tall white gateposts, and a double line of majestic poplars led the way to the trim lawns and the steps leading up to the massive oaken door of the four-square edifice.

In the month that had ensued since she

obtained the post, Amanda had settled her affairs in London, and was now looking forward to this complete change of life. She had always loved the country, and since her mother had died suddenly only three months earlier she had sensed that the only way to relieve the grief and shock was to make a complete break with the past. Now she was upon the threshold of that break, and the idea did not seem quite so good.

Alighting from the taxi, she waited while the driver unloaded her three cases, and a pang stabbed through her as she glanced at them, aware that they contained all her worldly possessions. She fought down the wave of emotion that tried to engulf her and paid the driver, thanking him for his service. As he touched his hat and departed she turned to survey the front of the house once more, and saw the front door open. A tall, lean man, dressed in a dark grey dust coat, appeared and descended the steps towards her, a welcoming smile on his craggy face. He wore a navy blue peaked cap, and she recognized him from her previous visit, although she could not remember his name. He was the porter, and she had gleaned that his wife was the cook here at the Hall.

'Good morning, Sister!' he greeted affably, smiling. 'Glad to see you. I was told to expect you. So here you are at last, and a nice day for travelling you've had.'

'I've only come from London,' responded Amanda, glancing around at the flat Essex countryside. 'But it is beautiful. The sunshine makes everywhere seem so different.'

'That's true.' He bent to pick up her cases. 'In case you've forgotten, my name is Woodley, Graham Woodley. Everyone around here, from the nurses to the Matron, call me Woody, so I'll answer to that if you ever need to address me.'

'Thank you, Woody!' Amanda smiled, and followed him as he ascended the steps. 'Have you been here long?'

'The Hall has been open as a nursing home for just over two years,' he replied. 'I came here from St Mark's hospital in

Hayley, where Doctor Ormond was working until he decided to open this place. I assume he told you something of the history of the Hall when you came down for your interview.'

'He didn't, actually,' she replied, glancing around as she stepped over the threshold into a large, tiled-floor hall, with a massive wooden staircase on the right. The hall was oak-panelled, and spotlessly clean. There were several doors in the wall beneath the staircase, and a corridor led off to the right, commencing at the foot of the stairs.

'Croxton Hall belongs to Doctor Ormond's father, who owns the neighbouring farm. Doctor Ormond spent a long time talking his father into letting him set up the Hall as a nursing home, but since he took over he certainly has worked wonders with the place. It was beginning to run to seed, but all that has been put right.' Woody started up the stairs. 'If you'll follow me, Sister, I'll show you to your apartment, and when you've unpacked and settled in you can come down and I'll take you to Matron. She'll probably take you round this afternoon. You won't be coming on duty until tomorrow.'

'Fine. Thank you.' Amanda drew a deep breath as they reached the first floor landing.

'We have patients on the ground floor and this first floor,' continued Woody, breathing heavily. 'All staff quarters are on the second floor and in the attics. The nurses have the attics. You have a nice apartment on the next floor. Matron has her apartment next to yours. I'm sure you'll be delighted with the place.'

'I'm certain I'll be happy here,' responded Amanda. 'I'm happy to get out of London. It was beginning to pall after the death of my mother.'

'You're all alone in the world now, so I heard. That's a hard thing to bear. But you're young. I don't want to pry, but isn't there a young man somewhere?'

'No.' Amanda smiled wryly. 'There was a

young man, as you put it, some years ago, but we drifted apart. Since then I've always found other things to do.'

'You'll get more free time here than you would in a large hospital,' said Woody, beginning to ascend the next flight of stairs. 'There are thirty-four patients, although we can accommodate fifty. Duties are split into three eight-hour shifts. There is a Sister on each shift, also a staff nurse and three nurses. You've already met Matron, and there's an assistant matron, Mrs Hargreaves. Doctor Ormond is always on call, of course. I've never known a man to work so hard. But this is his pet project and he wouldn't take time off even if he could. He's got to prove himself in the eyes of his father, who's given him three years to make the nursing home a viable proposition, as he calls it.'

Amanda digested all the information as they went on up to her room, and Woody led the way into her apartment. She had already seen the place on her first visit, and it suited her quite well. There was a sitting room, a bedroom and a bathroom, and the floor was carpeted, the furniture modern and of good quality.

'If there's anything you need then just let me know, although Matron has checked that everything is in order.' Woody put down her cases and stood surveying her features.

'Thank you. You're very kind,' she responded, crossing to a window and gazing out across the countryside. She saw flower gardens set in the lawns, and daffodils were bowing their yellow heads in the breeze. 'I'll unpack and then come down to see Matron. I need to know what shift I'll be taking over, and to familiarize myself with the Home.'

'If you feel like taking a walk this afternoon, if you like that kind of thing, then follow the path at the rear of the Home and leave through the kitchen gardens. There's a well defined footpath that crosses the fields to a ruined abbey. That's a sight well worth seeing.'

'I am interested in that sort of thing,' said

Amanda. 'Thank you. If I have the time I'll take the walk this afternoon.'

'You can't lose your way. Once you leave the kitchen gardens you follow a path until you come to a gate. Climb over the gate and follow the footpath.'

He turned to the door, and Amanda suppressed a sigh as she opened her handbag to find her keys. Unlocking the cases, she began the task of unpacking, and soon put her clothes into the wardrobe and drawers. Then she crossed to the window again, gazing reflectively at the scenery, and she knew this was the moment of truth. She had felt the need for a change and this was it. Now she had to settle to the fact.

A knock at the door startled her, and she turned swiftly to go in answer. When she opened the door she found herself confronted by Mrs Duncan, the matron, a medium-sized, plump woman about fifty, whose tightly waved hair was showing streaks of grey. She was dressed in a dark grey two-piece suit with a white blouse, and looked immaculate and business-like.

'Hello, Sister Wright,' she greeted, extending her hand. 'Woody told me you had arrived. I gave you time to unpack, but I thought I'd come and greet you just in case you were feeling a bit unsettled.'

'Thank you,' responded Amanda, smiling. 'I have just finished unpacking, and was planning to come down to locate you. I'm settling in just fine, and was just admiring the scenery.'

'I'll show you around now, if you like, and then it will be time for lunch. I've put you in charge of the seven-till-three shift starting from tomorrow morning. There are three shifts; the other two being from three-till-eleven and eleven-till-seven in the morning. They rotate every fortnight to give everyone a chance of different times off duty. Weekends are covered by temporary staff recruited locally – mainly married women who were nurses before marriage and who wish to earn part-time in order to augment their family income. But there are opportunities for anyone on the regular staff to work overtime on those weekend shifts.'

'I recall you explaining to me when I came down for the interview,' said Amanda. 'I'm quite happy about the working arrangements.'

They left the room and Mrs Duncan showed Amanda around the staff quarters. The rooms occupied by the nurses were on the next floor, and there were some Do Not Disturb notices on some of the doors.

'Night shift,' explained Mrs Duncan. 'That's why it's so quiet around here during the mornings. There is a strict rule about no noise.'

'Naturally,' agreed Amanda.

'Let's go down to the Sisters' office,' suggested Matron. 'And I have your two uniforms ready, based on the measurements you left with me. Perhaps you'll try them on today and ensure that they fit. Doctor Ormond will probably want to have another chat with you some time today about your duties, but he's always around and will see you when he can. Some of our patients have their own doctors to attend them, but the majority who come here place themselves under Doctor Ormond's care.'

Amanda listened to the information that was imparted as they descended to the ground floor, and she recalled Doctor Ormond from her first visit. He had been rather harassed, she recalled, and had a memory of a tall, powerful man of around thirty, with black hair and brown eyes, and a dimple in his left cheek. But she dragged herself from her thoughts as Matron led the way into the Sisters' Office.

'Sister Walters, this is Sister Wright,' introduced Mrs Duncan, and a tall, dark-haired woman in her thirties arose from the desk with a smile of welcome to shake Amanda's hand. She was dressed in a starched dark blue uniform and white cap, with white cuffs, and there was friendliness in her features.

'We did meet when you came for the interview,' recalled Sister Walters, and

Amanda agreed. 'I do hope you'll be happy here. Some of the staff find it difficult to settle down in these rural surroundings after the town.'

'Not me,' retorted Amanda. 'I prefer the country.'

'It's quite nice, especially with Spring upon us at last, although it is a bit forbidding in Winter,' said Matron.

The telephone rang and Sister Walters answered, then looked at Matron.

'That was Doctor Ormond, Matron,' she reported. 'He'd like to see you in his office when you have a moment.'

'I'll see him now,' responded Mrs Duncan. She smiled at Amanda. 'If you'll excuse me, Sister. Sister Walters will show you around and explain something of your duties.' She departed quickly, and Amanda regarded her colleague.

'I'm sure you'll like it here,' said Sister Walters. 'There's not so much discipline as you would expect in a hospital. We're just like one, big, happy family. Mind you, there are one or two on the staff who need watching, but I'll not influence you in any way. You'll soon discover which of your nurses you can rely on and who has to be watched. You're starting your duties in the morning, aren't you?'

'At seven,' agreed Amanda, glancing around the office. There was a large green filing cabinet behind the desk, which was covered with papers and diet sheets and some case histories. On one wall, high up and out of the way, was a glass-covered board with rows of indicators, numbered from one to fifty.

'Room numbers,' volunteered Sister Walters, noting Amanda's glance. 'Each one lights up, and there's a buzzer attached to attract your attention if you happen to be out of the office. You won't find it too busy, as it sometimes is in a hospital. We follow a strict routine, but it isn't daunting.'

'I've never been afraid of hard work,' commented Amanda.

Sister Walters smiled. 'You'll like Sister

Stewart, who is on nights this week. Assistant Matron, Mrs Hargreaves, is running the afternoon shift, which I shall take over tomorrow when you take over the morning shift from me. We've been working a bit short-handed since your predecessor departed, but everyone pulls her weight so it hasn't been too bad.'

'There are thirty-four patients at the moment, aren't there?' queried Amanda.

'That's right. All case histories are in the filing cabinet. There's a report book which must be kept up to date. Doctor Ormond keeps a case book himself, in his office. Generally, you'll find the administration run on the lines that you've been accustomed to in a hospital, so you won't be at all out of your depth. I'm about to make a round of the patients, so if you'd like to accompany me I'll show you where everyone is. You'll make a daily round with the doctor at least once during your shift, but he's always popping in to see one or another of the patients. This isn't an old people's home by any means, but the majority of our patients are elderly, mostly suffering from old age. We have visitors during the afternoons and evenings.'

Amanda nodded, and accompanied Sister Walters on a round of the patients, and by the time they returned to the office on the ground floor she was satisfied that she could handle the job with no problems. She would miss the bustle of hospital surroundings, but this was all to the good, and after Sister Walters had shown her the files in the big green cabinet she felt more relaxed, for this was the kind of work to which she was accustomed.

As she left the office she was confronted by Matron and Doctor Ormond, who extended a hand and smiled.

'Welcome to our family circle, Sister Wright,' he greeted. 'I do hope you'll be happy with us. If you have any problems at all then don't hesitate to consult either Matron or myself.'

'Thank you.' Amanda felt a tingle along

her spine as she shook his hand. He was tall and dark, as she remembered, and his regular features were attractive. The dimple was showing in his left cheek as he smiled, but she noted that his brown eyes seemed to be shadowed by intangible worries.

He excused himself and departed hurriedly, and Matron shook her head as she gazed after him.

'I feel so sorry for him,' she declared in low tones. 'He's almost killing himself in an attempt to prove to his father that he can make this place pay. Croxton Hall used to be the Ormond family home until Doctor Ormond persuaded his father to let him open it as a nursing home. The doctor's father, Charles Ormond, has the neighbouring farm, and he is against this project, although he has not put any barriers in Doctor Ormond's way.'

'That's why he looks so harassed,' observed Amanda.

'So you've noticed.' Matron nodded and smiled gently. 'I think he will prove his point, but his father is a rather forceful man. We have had some trouble with him – nurses trespassing upon his land, so he claims, although there is a public footpath across his fields to the ruined abbey, and he can't keep anyone off by law.'

'And I'm sure no nurse is going to commit a nuisance or cause damage,' added Amanda.

Matron smiled. 'That's the trouble, I believe. Doctor Ormond's father is looking for reasons why the nursing home should be closed but cannot find any. Now I must be about my duties. Are you quite happy so far, Sister? If there is anything you want to know then don't hesitate to ask questions. All of the staff here will be eager to help you settle in.'

'Thank you, Matron. I'm sure I shall cope. I'll be ready for duty at seven in the morning. I'd better try my uniforms now, in case they need any minor alterations.'

'Then I'll see you when you take up your duties. I wish you well, Sister, and I hope you'll be very happy here.'

Amanda smiled, and Mrs Duncan left her. For a moment Amanda stood thinking about the situation, but could not find any problems, and went up to her room. A nurse was coming down the stairs, and she paused, smiling.

'I'm Sister Wright,' volunteered Amanda. 'If you're on morning shift then we shall be working together as from tomorrow.'

'I'm Stacey Fleming, Sister. I shall be working with you. I'm pleased to meet you, and I hope you'll find it pleasant here.'

'Thank you, Nurse. I'll find it a bit strange at first, but I'll soon settle in. Have you been here long?'

'About five months now, and I don't regret the day I left general hospital work for this routine. Have you met any of the others who will be on our shift?'

'No. I've spoken to Matron, and Woody, the porter. I've also seen Sister Walters.'

'There's Staff Nurse Brant – Thelma Brant – Nurse Everard and Nurse Clayton on your shift, Sister. They're busy with the patients at the moment, I expect. I've just finished my break.'

'Then don't let me delay you,' responded Amanda. 'I'll be seeing you in the morning, Nurse.'

They parted, and Amanda went on up to her room, her mind filled with the host of new impressions she had gained. It would take some getting used to the change of tempo in the nursing home, compared with what she had experienced in a hospital, but her colleagues seemed a decent crowd, and she expected to get along well with them.

She had lunch in a large dining room, and sat with Sister Walters, who was taking a break. They chatted generally, and Amanda found her liking for her surroundings strengthening. After lunch she went out to investigate the surrounding grounds, and followed a path through the kitchen gardens, letting herself out to the countryside beyond by way of a thick wooden gate set in a high wall.

Before her lay the fields, and a footpath stretched away beside a leafy hedge towards a distant copse. She heard a pheasant call, and high overhead the sound of a passing aircraft marred the serenity of the scene. Amanda felt herself losing touch with reality as she followed the path, trying to recall Woody's instructions for reaching the ruined abbey. The afternoon sun was warm upon her shoulders, and she carried her cardigan.

When she came to a five-barred gate in the hedge she recalled Woody's instructions and remembered the country code. Never leave farm gates open. The words formed in her mind, but when she looked at the gate she found a chain around it which was padlocked into position. But Woody had told her to climb the gate and continue along the footpath beyond.

Peering over the gate, she failed to see any footpath, but began to clamber over the gate, careful not to dirty her pale pink skirt. She paused atop the gate and inspected the field. There was a cow in knee-deep grass and buttercups, and as she jumped down inside the field the animal looked up. Amanda paused uncertainly, eyeing the beast warily. Being town-bred, she had a healthy respect for any animal that was larger than a dog, and she took a tentative step forward from the gate.

Somewhere in the distance a man's voice sounded, echoing many times in a shout. She glanced around, but could see no one, and began resolutely to cross the field, her eyes upon the large black and white cow. The animal was still looking at her intently, then turned slowly to face her. Amanda paused, frowning as she took in the heavily-built head and short, thick horns. Was it a cow or a bull? She could not tell, but when the beast began to move towards her, slowly at first, then at a run, she became alarmed and turned to run back to the gate, surprised that she had covered so many yards from it. When she glanced over her shoulder she was greatly alarmed to see the animal bearing down upon her, its hooves pounding the long grass.

At first Amanda thought she would not be able to reach the gate before the animal reached her, and fear was vibrant in her mind. She glanced backwards again, certain now that the animal was a bull, and then she was against the gate and scrambling over the bars, flinging herself to the safety of the footpath. There was a crashing sound that forced her to spring up, and she saw the bull on the other side of the gate, sounding like a steam train as it struck at the wooden barrier with its powerful head.

Trembling with shock, Amanda eyed the animal, fearful that it might batter its way through the gate. The next instant she heard approaching feet, and glanced around to see a tall, lean man hurrying towards her, a shotgun under his right arm. A black and white collie was at his heels, seeming to slink over the ground.

'Stupid girl!' shouted the man, who was well into middle age. 'Didn't you hear me call?' He came up to her, pausing to peer into her pale face and narrowed blue eyes. 'I suppose you're another of those nurses from the hall, eh? You've no right to be out alone if you don't know the difference between a cow and a bull. I assume you wouldn't willingly go into a field where a stock bull is standing, would you?'

'I certainly didn't know it was a bull!' replied Amanda, angered by his manner and brusqueness. 'It's a dangerous animal, and there should be a notice up to that effect.'

Her words cut short his flow, and for a moment he was startled, but his dark eyes glinted and he sighed heavily.

'This happens to be private property.'

'I was told to follow the footpath from the Hall and cross the gate to follow the footpath to the ruined abbey. I understand that there is a right of way. And isn't it against the law to put a dangerous animal in a field where there is a right of way?'

'The footpath doesn't cross this particular field,' he retorted. 'It's the next gate along that you should have used. I spotted you climbing this gate and shouted. Are you deaf?'

'I did hear a voice, but it was a long way off.'

'I had to run to get here, and even then I was too late.' He glanced down at the shotgun he was carrying. 'I would have been even angrier if I'd been forced to shoot that prize bull just to save you from your rashness.' He brushed past her and patted the bull's nose, talking soothingly to the irate animal.

'It doesn't look at all dangerous now,' commented Amanda in some surprise.

'He's not, so long as there's a gate between you. But the instant you enter his territory then look out for trouble. Who are you, young lady? Are you from the Hall?'

'Yes, I am. I arrived today to take up my duties as a nursing Sister.'

'I see,' he growled, glancing at her. 'Well you've had a very dangerous introduction to the countryside. It's quite plain that you have no knowledge of our way of life.'

'I took this position because I like the country, and one has to start learning at some time in one's life. You're a country-man, but I suspect that your father began to teach you at an early age.'

'I'm Charles Ormond, and my son talked me into letting him convert the Hall into a nursing home much to my regret. So you're a fully qualified nurse, are you?'

'Yes, Mr Ormond.'

'Has anyone warned you against me?' he demanded.

'No. Why should they? Do you bite?' Amanda could not resist the barb. She had been frightened out of her life, and his attitude had shown no consideration. To her surprise he smiled thinly.

'My bark is worse than my bite,' he said slowly. 'So you want to see the ruined abbey, do you? Would you mind some company? I haven't been up that way for more years than I care to remember. I'll show you the way, if you like.'

'Thank you. That's very kind of you.'
Amanda spoke cautiously, aware of what
Matron had told her of this man's attitude
to Doctor Ormond's project. She did not
want to make matters any worse for her new
employer, and thought it would be
diplomatic to humour this important
person. 'If you're sure I'm not being a
nuisance and a trespasser then I'd
appreciate your company.'

He chuckled again. 'Come along then, and
don't make the mistake of trying to pat my
dog. She's a working dog, and she'd have
your fingers off, as like as not, if you reached
out to her.'

Amanda stifled a sigh and fell into step at
his side as he walked on along the path. She
felt a strange sense of disquiet in the back of
her mind, for the future of the entire
nursing home seemed to rest in this man's
hands, and she felt that she ought to
humour him as far as possible. When he
began to talk about the locality she listened
intently, wanting to learn something about

the area in which she intended to live, and she found him interesting despite the way in which they had met. He warmed to her company as they followed the footpath, and Amanda began to tell him something of her past and background. By the time they reached the ruined abbey the shock and the hard feelings had passed from between them and they were chatting as if they had been friends for years.

TWO

'You should have had my son bring you out here,' said Charles Ormond, after Amanda had inspected the grey ruins that arose somewhat haphazardly from the long grass. 'He knows a great deal about the history of this place. For myself, they're just a pile of rubble that's a nuisance to a farmer. I'm not one for history. It's the present and the future that concern me. But my boy is something of a dreamer, worse luck.'

'Surely not!' exclaimed Amanda. 'The fact that he's founded the nursing home proves he's someone who gets things done.'

'That's true, especially in view of the fact that I've put as many obstacles as possible in his way. But the Hall was our family seat for generations. Now it's cluttered up with a lot of strangers. The Ormonds were proud of their history of hospitality. But now the place is filled with paying guests.'

'They're patients, not guests,' countered Amanda.

'You people are all the same. Mrs Duncan talks just like you. I suspect you all come out of the same mould. But I can't for the life of me figure out why my son had to take up with this sort of thing.'

'You don't like him being a doctor?' questioned Amanda.

'I've got nothing against that. It's an honourable profession. But he should have taken a general practice somewhere, or carried on with his work in a hospital, as he set out to do.'

'He must feel that he's doing more good with a nursing home,' affirmed Amanda.

'You people all stick together.' Charles Ormond turned and looked into her face, his dark eyes bright and searching. 'I must say that you sound like a sharp, efficient nurse. You're just the type Richard needs around him, not the kind who tried to lead him up the garden path.'

'I'd rather not hear anything about Doctor Ormond's private life,' rebuked Amanda, and saw his face darken.

'You say you arrived today, eh? When do you start your duties?'

'Tomorrow morning at seven.'

'Then would you do me the honour of having tea with me this afternoon? I made a rule never to associate with any of my son's staff, but as you haven't taken up your duties yet you don't come under that classification. I've been in a strange mood all day, and I think life is beginning to turn sour on me. But talking to you seems to have lifted the gloom somewhat. Would you do an old man a great favour?'

'Thank you, but I'm wondering what Doctor Ormond might say about it.'

'It has nothing to do with him. In any case he's always too busy to spend any time with me. I think he works twenty-four hours a day in the Hall. That's partly why I'm hoping he'll fail in this venture of his. God knows a doctor works long hours as it is, but he seems to do the work of two men.'

'And you haven't been making it easy for him,' observed Amanda.

'That's true, but then I think it is a test of character if a man has to fight for what he wants. Now what about tea? I might add that there are some of your colleagues who would give a great deal to receive such an invitation, if only to have the opportunity to try and persuade me to come over on my son's side. But you're a new arrival, and I don't think that side of it would affect you at this time.'

'Doctor Ormond certainly has my loyalty right from the start.'

'Very well then. Accept my offer to tea and you may try to make me see this situation from the nursing point of view.'

'Thank you. Perhaps I may be able to do that.' Amanda smiled, for she had already come to the conclusion that this old man's bark was worse than his bite.

'My wife is dead,' he said as they left the ruins and followed a different footpath. They were on high ground at that moment, and Amanda could see the solid building of the Hall to the left. To the right of it was a large, red-roofed farm house, surrounded by trees, and in the background were a number of barns and other buildings. 'She died of cancer of the lung. You wouldn't have thought that, would you? She never smoked in her life and spent all her years in the fresh air of this district.'

'Is that why you're feeling such animosity towards the medical profession?' queried Amanda.

'No.' He shook his head, his dark eyes glittering as he glanced at her. 'Don't think that. I am a fatalist. I accept whatever comes along. My antipathy towards what my son is doing with the Hall, although I gave consent in the first place, stems from the fact that it is the ancestral home, so to speak, and I can't abide all those strangers around. Those nurses, when they're off duty, come tramping through the fields. They don't stay on the footpaths, and some of their boy-friends trespass at night. Then there's the incident of your confrontation with my bull.'

'You can't lay the blame for that at my door,' retorted Amanda firmly, meeting his gaze as he glanced at her. 'A public footpath passes that gate, and you should have a notice up stating that there's a bull in the field. Anyone could have mistaken that gateway for the right one.'

'I don't know why I'm in such a forgiving mood this afternoon,' he countered, 'but I'll take your point. Come along, let's cut across here and through the woods. I'll give you a nature study lesson on the way to the farm.' He glanced down at her feet. 'At least you have the good sense to wear the proper type of shoe. I've seen some of your colleagues hobbling around on stiletto heels! I don't know why my son brings them in. He should have local girls.'

'Perhaps there are no local girls who are capable nurses,' defended Amanda. 'Anyway, I heard that the week-end staff are recruited from local women.'

They followed a path that led into a woods, and Amanda looked around with interest, taking note of everything that Charles Ormond explained to her. He pointed out a blackbird's nest, and showed her the five bluish-green eggs that it contained. A pigeon's nest, consisting of nothing more than a sparse platform of twigs, had three white eggs on its precarious perch. Then there was a pheasant's nest in a clump of undergrowth, and she saw at least eighteen khaki-coloured eggs clustered together.

Charles Ormond appreciated her real interest, and smiled condescendingly at her exclamations of amazement as she saw the everyday country-side sights that were new to her wide blue eyes. He suddenly snapped his shotgun closed and lifted the weapon to his shoulder. Amanda flinched at the heavy detonation that rang out and reverberated through the woods, clapping her hands to her ears, and she frowned as she watched a rook tumbling out of the sky. He glanced at her, smiling grimly.

'Death strikes all the time in the country,' he said. 'Amidst all this beauty there are ugly scenes. It might be a stoat after a rabbit or a hawk after a sparrow, but it goes on, and I liken it to living in a big city.'

Amanda's ears were ringing from the shock of the shot, and she swallowed to clear her head. She sighed as she considered, and had to admit that he seemed biased against the different way of life which had crept to within his home. The suburbs had evidently sprawled outwards from the town in recent years, and his son had turned the ancestral Hall into a nursing home, bringing in strangers and their visitors. No doubt some people did abuse the surrounding farm land, and Amanda could sympathize with him. When she told him as much she saw him nod, and something akin to respect showed in his expression.

'I wish Richard had found himself someone like you,' he commented as they passed out of the wood and began to approach the big farm house by the rushing stream. 'The girl he brought home a few years ago was city bred, and hated the country-side. She didn't like me and was against the idea of turning the Hall into a nursing home. I agreed with her there, of course, and it was the only thing we could agree about. But her objections were personal. She wanted to live in the Hall and act like the lady of the Manor. I was relieved when Richard broke off his engagement and sent her packing.'

'I don't think you should talk about my employer in that way,' protested Amanda.

'Nonsense!' He brushed aside her protests. 'He's my son, and I can say what I like so long as it is the truth.'

Amanda looked around with mounting interest as they reached the farm yard, where a paved area gave access to stables. A man wearing a red shirt and riding breeches appeared from the doorway of one of the stables, and gazed in some surprise at Amanda, but Charles Ormond merely motioned to the dog, which had kept silent at their heels all the time, and it moved off obediently towards the man in the doorway.

'Take care of Patch, William,' ordered Charles Ormond, and removed the cartridges from his shotgun, pocketing them and leading Amanda towards the rear of the house.

'This is a beautiful place,' observed Amanda.

'Looking at it through a city-bred person's eyes, I suppose it is, but this is a place of work, and the scenery doesn't mean a thing to anyone brought up in its midst. Let's go through the kitchen and I can tell Mrs Harmsworth that I have a guest for tea.'

He led the way into a large, sandstone-paved kitchen, and a tall, grey-haired woman turned to look at them. Her wrinkled face showed some surprise at the sight of Amanda, but she quickly composed herself and awaited instructions.

'This is Sister Wright, Mrs Harmsworth,' explained Charles Ormond. 'I met her looking over the property. She's new at the Hall. I've asked her to stay to tea. Will you see to it at the right time?'

'Certainly.' A smile crossed the woman's face. 'How do you do, Sister? There must be something special about you. I've never known Mr Ormond to invite even the Matron here to tea.'

'I came upon her entering the field where I've got the bull,' retorted Charles Ormond. 'There was almost a nasty incident. I'll have to get a sign put up by that gate. She isn't the first one to mistake the gateway for the one giving access to the footpath. I'll just pop along to my study and put away the shotgun. Then I'll show you around the house, Sister.' He motioned to the house-keeper. 'Mrs Harmsworth will keep you occupied until I return.'

Amanda nodded, and remained silent until he had departed. Then she looked at Mrs Harmsworth, who smiled knowingly.

'I'd say that you stood up to him when he bullied you!'

'We did have a slight altercation,' admitted Amanda. 'But he appears to be a man accustomed to getting his own way.'

'He's certainly that. I feel sorry for Doctor Ormond. Things could have been made a lot easier for him, but he has to stand up to his father all the time. It's a constant battle between them. Did you know Doctor Ormond before coming here?'

'No. I met him when I came for an inter-view about five weeks ago. But I knew I'd like to work here as soon as I saw the place. I didn't understand that there was trouble though.'

'It's just a family matter. But you can take it from me that Mr Ormond isn't as hard as he makes out. He's still suffering the effects of losing Mrs Ormond.'

'He told me about her.' Amanda nodded. 'I think he's quite nice, if you look beneath the exterior.'

'Well you must have made an instant impression upon him, because I've never known him to ask anyone in for tea before. Would you like a cup of tea now?'

'If it wouldn't be too much trouble.'

'No trouble at all. I was about to make a pot of tea anyway. I expect Mr Ormond will have one. Have you been in the country before?'

'No. I've been a city dweller.' Amanda smiled. 'But I'm looking forward to this. I've always had a yearning for the country. My mother was a country girl.' She began to explain her circumstances and the events leading up to her decision to apply for the vacant position at the Hall, and Mrs Harmsworth listened with interest.

Then Charles Ormond returned, and Amanda accompanied him to the big sitting room. Age-blackened beams were low overhead, and she looked around observantly, aware that Charles Ormond was watching for her reaction.

'This is a beautiful room,' she said firmly.

'It's missing the woman's touch these days,' he responded. 'But it was my wife's favourite room, and she kept it spotless. I'm not saying that Mrs Harmsworth doesn't keep it clean, but there's been something lacking since my wife died.'

'I can understand what you mean,' responded Amanda. 'I felt the same way after my mother died. It's something you've got to experience before you can understand it.'

'Exactly.' He nodded, and for a moment this face was set in harsh lines. 'But please sit down and make yourself at home. You're a different person altogether to the girl my son brought home.' He paused and smiled thinly. 'There I go again. I'll have to watch my tongue when Richard is around or I'll give him cause for another argument.'

'He looked rather harassed when I met him this morning,' said Amanda.

'My fault entirely. I was having a go at him earlier about the state of the grounds around the Hall. But I suppose he has enough on his plate with the interior of the place, so I'm going to get my gardeners to take over the grounds. That will relieve him of some of the pressure.'

Amanda seated herself in a chair by the window, and could see part of the Hall from her position. They chatted generally until Mrs Harmswoth tapped at the door and entered with a large tray, which she set upon a table.

'Leave it, Mrs Harmsworth,' instructed Charles Ormond. 'I'm sure Sister Wright is capable of pouring tea for the both of us.' He smiled as the housekeeper departed. 'Don't keep us waiting too long for tea, will you?' he asked as the door closed.

'I'll have it ready for four-fifteen,' came the

firm reply as Mrs Harmsworth departed.

Amanda arose and poured tea into two cups, handing one to her host, and he thanked her in husky tones and leaned back in his seat. When she had reseated herself he nodded slowly.

'You may wonder why I invited you here today,' he began slowly. 'Truth to tell, I'm wondering what is in the back of my mind. But I am getting tired of the constant bickering that goes on between me and my son. But I'm not going to back down. It's something I've never done in my life. But you could prove to be a great help. I'd like for you to become a regular visitor here, and in return for that favour I will make life a great deal easier for everyone at the Hall. What do you say to that?'

'How can I refuse, if it is for the good of my colleauges?' countered Amanda. 'But how would you use me in this situation?'

'You're perceptive, I'll grant that.' He chuckled, and his brown eyes glinted as he gazed at her. 'But all I want is for you to act as a buffer between us. Richard works far too hard and I think that if I bring in an outsider, an entirely new face, I might be able to ease off the pressure I've applied under the excuse that you have helped me see matters in a different light.'

'I don't know exactly what the situation has been here,' she said slowly. 'But I'm prepared to help in any way I can, just so long as you're not attempting to use me differently to the way you are suggesting.'

'Such as?'

'Instead of using me to help the situation from Doctor Ormond's point of view you try to do the opposite in order to gain a further advantage.' Amanda's voice was pitched low and evenly.

'I promise that I wouldn't do that,' he said, lifting his right hand. 'I really have my son's interests at heart, and he's so set upon making a success of this business that I have to respect his ideas. I'll do what I can to help him, but the change in my attitude must appear to be slow and obvious. Help me to achieve that and I'll come round to Richard's way of thinking.'

'All right. Under those conditions, I'll agree to what you ask,' she replied.

'Good. So you like the country, do you?' He changed the subject abruptly. 'You might change your mind if you had to get up early on a Winter morning to turn out and do the milking. But this time of year is beautiful. Can you ride? I have several horses in my stables.'

'No. The only thing I've ridden is a bicycle.'

'Would you care to learn?' he demanded, smiling.

'I don't know. I might be afraid of horses. After the episode with your bull I'm going to have a very healthy respect for any kind of animal. You even warned me against your dog.'

'Patch wouldn't bit you. I was only joking. But she is a working dog and I don't like people patting her or making a fuss of her because she isn't a pet. That's why I said she's likely to bite.'

Amanda shook her head ruefully. 'If you think you need an excuse to get me here, for your son's benefit, then I'll take a chance and agree to trying to learn to ride.'

'Capital! It's just the excuse we need. I'll mention it to Richard when I see him. He's going to get a shock when he discovers that you've been here to tea. Every time I see him I moan about those nurses.'

'I'm still trying to puzzle out why you've changed your attitude since meeting me,' said Amanda.

'I've been looking for an excuse to change my attitude, and you seem to have come along to step into the breach. Let's leave it at that, shall we?'

'Certainly.' Amanda began to drink her tea. 'I think I'm getting the best of the deal. I'll be able to observe the country-side at first hand, and enjoy the rural pursuits under your patronage. But some of my colleagues may turn envious when they discover what's happening.'

'I'll relent slowly, and give them permission to use the place, if they're considerate. I can't say fairer than that.'

Amanda nodded, and they chatted amicably until Mrs Harmsworth opened the door and wheeled in a trolley laden with tea. The housekeeper smiled at Amanda, and there was still a trace of surprise in her face, as if she could not really believe that her master had relented at all from his previously obdurate position. Amanda had some misgivings about Charles Ormond's real reasons for taking this particular stand, but she could only wait and see how events developed.

They were halfway through tea when the door was opened and Doctor Ormond entered the room. Amanda glanced up at the sound of the door, a cucumber sandwich in her hand, and she was almost as surprised as Richard Ormond himself. He halted and stared at her with widening brown eyes as a silence developed.

'Well don't stand there with your mouth

open, Richard,' said Charles Ormond with a harsh edge to his tone. 'Either come in and join us or apologize for interrupting us and clear off.'

'Sister Wright,' said Richard Ormond, coming in and closing the door.

'That's what she said her name is.' Charles Ormond launched into a narrative of how he had met Amanda, and she realized that he was colouring the story slightly but did not contradict him. 'I shall have to put up a notice in that field to prevent a tragedy. Those nurses of yours run around the fields as if they're in the heart of the city. They don't seem to realize that a farm is a very dangerous place.'

'I've warned all of them to stay well clear of the farm,' replied Richard, still gazing at Amanda. 'But Sister Wright only arrived this morning and I didn't get the opportunity to do more than say hello to her. I really ought to have taken the time to warn her of the dangers. If anything had happened to her I would have had it on my conscience for the rest of my life.'

'Well you can make amends for your lapse by escorting her back to the Hall when she's ready to go.' The rough edge was still in the older man's tone, but Amanda was aware that he was bluffing. 'The least I could do after the fright she had was bring her back here. She was grey with shock.' His right eyelid flickered slightly as Amanda instinctively opened her mouth to deny his statement, and she lapsed into silence. 'But I must admit that I've quite enjoyed her company. Having her to talk to has made me realise there's more to life than arguing with you every time you show your face around here, Richard. See to it that Sister Wright comes over here whenever she wants to visit.' He paused and fixed Amanda with a steady gaze. 'Can't we forget the formalities a bit?' he demanded. 'Why should I have to call you Sister Wright after saving your life? What's your name? You're not a plain Jane or an ordinary Mary, are you?'

'I'm Amanda,' she replied, trying to keep a

straight face and preserve the atmosphere he had deliberately created.

'Amanda!' Charles Ormond nodded slowly. 'A nice, substantial name. 'Well, may I call you Amanda?'

'Please do!' She nodded, aware that Richard Ormond was gazing at his father with wonderment stamped upon his features.

'Fine. Well I've got some business to attend to now, Amanda, so I'm sure you'll excuse me. Richard will tell you that I don't usually socialize at all. He'll have tea with you, and then see you safely back to the Hall again. But don't forget. I'd like to see you here again, and you can make full use of anything on the farm. Richard, Amanda has expressed a desire to attempt to ride, so make sure you find the time to give her a lesson or two. She'll know in the first half hour if she'd take to it.'

'Certainly, Father.' Richard came to sit down as Charles Ormond arose and walked to the door. 'Anything you say.'

Amanda saw that there was a gulf between father and son, and she felt a thrill of anticipation when she realized that she had come upon the scene as if fate had intended her to be a mediator. Looking at Richard Ormond's handsome face, she felt a sense of intuition at work in her mind, and could only wonder exactly what was in store for her.

THREE

'I don't know what to say, Sister,' commented Richard Ormond as Amanda poured him a cup of tea. His brown eyes were filled with shock. 'Whether it's your personality or my father falling into senile decay I don't know, but he's never invited even Mrs Duncan here to tea. I almost had a heart attack when I came in and saw you here.'

'I'm in a mild state of shock myself,' responded Amanda, smiling. 'I was frightened by the bull, and your father was almost offensive when he came to my rescue.' She did not explain the true facts of the incidents, wishing to preserve the atmosphere that Charles Ormond had created. 'But he had every right to be angry with me. Only an idiot would have willingly entered a field which contained a bull. But it was ignorance, and that is no excuse. I suspect that any animosity your father feels towards the nursing staff stems from their ignorance of the country code.'

'There's more to it than that,' he admitted. 'But I do know Father has been incensed by some of the incidents involving members of the staff.'

'He did mention something about boyfriends of the nursing staff trespassing.'

'But he only uses that as an excuse to get at me.' Richard sighed heavily. 'You may not be aware of it, Sister, but my father is dead set against the Hall being used as a nursing home, although he gave me permission in the first place to set it up. He hasn't made life easy for me, and could have helped a great deal if he had wanted to. But you seem to have gained a foothold here, and I'm wondering if I could ask you to try and capitalize upon it. I don't want you to do anything underhand, you understand. But please follow up his invitation. If he has taken a liking to you then it may be the thin end of the wedge for me. He may come round to my way of thinking if he finds that not all the nurses are intruders with no common sense or consideration.'

'I'll certainly do what I can, Doctor,' she responded, and felt an impulse to set his mind at rest by telling him exactly what Charles Ormond had suggested to her. She could see by his expression that he was strained almost to breaking point, and sympathy for him loomed in her thoughts. But she realized that the gulf between father and son would need careful tending if it were to heal naturally, and that was what

Charles Ormond wanted. It would have to be handled according to his rules, and she was prepared to go along with them.

'That's very kind of you, I don't know what you must be thinking of us, this being your first day. I would have spared you a meeting with my father, for he can be outrageous in his manner.' He smiled faintly. 'Yet you seemed to have tamed him. I had a feeling about you when you came for the interview last month. I think I did the right thing by selecting you from the short list we had compiled.'

'I hope you did the right thing, having burned my boats behind me,' Amanda responded.

'Don't worry. I'm sure you'll like the place when you've settled in. Get your first week of duty over and you'll be able to consider the situation more clearly. At least, you have shown a liking for the country.' His tone hardened a little. 'You'd be surprised at the number of females who suddenly decide that they miss the bright lights, even after stating a preference for the simplicity of a rustic way of life.'

Amanda knew he was thinking of his former fiancé, recalling his father's words, and she suppressed a sigh as she selected another cucumber sandwich.

'I don't think you'll have any problems with me in that respect,' she said. 'My mother died three months ago, and I'm all alone in the world. I love the country, and living-in at the Hall solves a number of problems. As Matron said, the staff live as one big happy family, so I shan't be lonely.'

'And my father has given you the freedom of the place!' His eyes gleamed for a moment, and his smile broadened. 'What a stroke of luck. We've really got to push this to the limit. You will come over here when you're off duty, won't you? Use the horse riding as an excuse. I'll make the time to teach you to ride. As Father said, the first half hour will indicate whether or not you like riding.'

'I'm ready to do anything that will help.' Amanda smiled, aware of the humour in the situation because she was in a position to view both sides, and she could understand Charles Ormond's attitude as well as his son's. 'But I've come here to work, and that must come first.'

'From your point of view it may seem imperative that you do your duty, but I assure that that this other side of the matter is just as important at the moment. If my father decides that I've had long enough to prove myself I may find that I'm closing down before I've had a real chance.'

'I think I understand.' Amanda nodded. She looked into his face, and saw that some of the stress had faded. She smiled. 'I didn't know what to expect before I arrived. You know how it is starting a new job. But even my wildest dreams didn't encompass this situation. I have to act as a peacemaker.'

'Would you really mind?' he countered. 'It's for the good of the nursing home, and you are now a member of the staff.'

'I don't mind at all. In fact, it seems to be quite a challenge. And I shall look forward to a riding lesson.'

'Perhaps you won't feel so eager after having been astride one of the horses,' he warned, and when he laughed there was genuine amusement in his tone. Amanda noted that he seemed five years younger when he lost his serious expression.

'Let me get my first duty shift behind me before we talk of other things,' she pleaded.

'I think we're going to get along very well,' he observed. 'In fact, we've got to, by all accounts. I've never known my father to ease in his position, but you've managed to get through his guard.'

'Perhaps I'd better not push my luck too hard,' she countered. 'I think I ought to be getting back to the Hall.'

'You're not on duty this evening,' he reminded her. 'You don't have to go back. I'm due for an evening off, so if you'd like me to show you around then I'd be only too happy to oblige.'

'That's very kind of you, considering how hard pressed you are at the moment. I have made no plans for this evening, except to make sure everything is ready for the morning.'

'That merely entails laying out your uniform, doesn't it?'

'Yes.' Amanda smiled as she nodded.

'Then let me show you some hospitality and take you for a meal this evening. I'll walk you back to the Hall if you'd like to change, but it would give me a reason for going out. I wouldn't bother otherwise, and everyone keeps telling me how hard I'm working and how I should have an evening off once in a while.'

'Would this attire be suitable for an evening in Frampton?' she asked, and saw his nod of approval. 'Then I accede to your invitation. It's very kind of you.'

'Not at all.' He paused, and for a moment there was query in his eyes. 'There isn't a boy-friend somewhere, is there? I wouldn't want that kind of complication.'

'No boy-friend.' She smiled, and saw him relax.

'Fine.' He glanced at his watch. 'It's early yet, so would you like to look around the farm? It might help if Father saw that I was taking his instructions seriously. He may just be testing me, you know.'

'In what way?' demanded Amanda wonderingly.

'If I ignore his wishes he might tighten up on me; increase the pressure. I've got to keep on his right side.'

'I've heard some reasons why I ought to go out on a date, but yours is the best one yet,' she responded, smiling.

'I didn't mean it to sound like that.' He smiled ruefully. 'What must you think of me?'

'It's all right. I understand.' Amanda nodded. 'I'd like a guided tour of the farm. I've never had the opportunity to look over one before.'

'Come along then.' He arose eagerly, and Amanda set down her cup and joined him.

He opened the door for her and ushered her to the kitchen, glancing around as he did so, but there was no sign of his father, and Amanda wondered if Charles Ormond was watching them, having gone to so much trouble to arrange the whole affair.

'Hello, Doctor,' greeted Mrs Harmsworth. 'Would you like some tea?'

'No thank you. I'm going to show Sister Wright around the farm.' He paused and glanced at Amanda. 'Do we have to be so formal off duty?' he demanded. 'If my father can call you Amanda surely you'll extend the favour to me.'

Amanda nodded, smiling, and saw the expression which came to the housekeeper's face. 'Certainly,' she agreed.

'And you must call me Richard. I'm tired of being called Doctor all the time. Even Mrs Harmsworth calls me doctor these days.'

'I can remember the time I used to call you Master Richard,' responded the housekeeper. 'But since you qualified I've been proud to call you doctor.'

He smiled and opened the back door. 'If they call for me from the Hall I'll be somewhere around the yards,' he said. 'Come along, Amanda.'

She went with him, and there was a strange feeling in her mind, as if reality had slipped away from them. From the moment she had realized she was in danger in that field fate seemed to have taken her firmly by the hand and propelled her into a situation which gripped her more tightly with each development. There was evidently no escape for her, and she accepted the situation and decided to make the best of it.

Richard showed her around the farm, which she found interesting, and afterwards took her into Frampton, which was a fairly large country town. Before they went to a restaurant he walked her along a tow path, and she saw ducks and swans upon the river. A number of cabin cruisers were moving sluggishly along the waterway, indicating that Summer was not far off, and the evening was warm and sunny. The breeze was cool, but Amanda wore her cardigan, and realized that she had not felt so relaxed for weeks.

Later, after a meal, she realized with a pang of disappointment that they had to return to the Hall. Richard had telephoned before they left the farm to leave a note of his movements, but he had not been summoned. But she knew how he was tied to the nursing home, and there was a great deal of sympathy for him in her mind. He drove her back to the Hall in dying sunlight, and when the car was halted in front of the large building Amanda was sorry that the day had come to an end.

'This has been a day of revelation,' he commented as they alighted from the car. 'When I awoke this morning I didn't know things would develop as they have done. I feel easier in my mind, knowing that you will be on my side, and on the inside with my father. I wonder what came over him! I've never known him to let his guard down. You're evidently someone out of the ordinary as far as he is concerned, and I'm keeping my fingers crossed in the hope that he won't revert to type after a few days. You will come across to the farm when you're off duty, won't you, to press home this advantage?'

'Certainly. I'll be off duty tomorrow afternoon. I'll try not to be too pushing, but I'll make my presence known.'

'If you can sway my father into taking a different attitude towards the nursing home then I'll be for ever in your debt,' he said fervently, and the dimple was in his left cheek as he smiled. 'I think fate has sent you here to help me out in more ways than one, Amanda.' He used her name in casual tone, and she glanced at him as they ascended the steps to the door of the Hall. His face was relaxed and she could tell that the tension had faded from his mind. But the time they had spent together seemed to have eased the strangeness from between them, and he was like an old friend now. He grinned at her as their glances met, and when Woody opened the door to them he greeted the porter affably.

'Glad to see you back, Doctor,' said the older man. 'Sister Stewart would like to see you. Nothing serious, but she is finding cause for concern in Mrs West's condition. She asked me to inform you the moment you arrived.'

'If you'll excuse me.' He turned to her, and Amanda began to nod, but he shook his head. 'You haven't met Sister Stewart yet. Perhaps you'd care to come along to the office.'

'Yes, certainly,' responded Amanda, and walked at his side along the corridor to the right. She saw a nurse walking along the corridor ahead of them, and light was issuing through the open doorway of the office. When they reached the office Amanda saw the blonde head of a fat, middle-aged woman bent over some reports on the desk, and the dark blue of a Sister's uniform covered the obese figure.

'You wanted to see me, Sister?' asked Richard, and Sister Stewart started and looked up quickly, relief showing in her fleshy features.

'Yes, Doctor. I'm glad you've returned. I have a feeling that all is not well with Mrs West. You asked me to let you know if there were any changes in her condition, and I think she has stopped making progress since I came on duty.'

'I'll go and take a look at her,' he responded, glancing at Amanda. 'This is Amanda Wright,' he introduced. 'Heather Stewart. I'll leave you together to get acquainted, and I'll be back in a few minutes.'

Amanda nodded, and went forward to shake the hand that Heather Stewart held out to her.

'I'd heard of your arrival, Amanda. I hope you'll like it here. But rumours get around very quickly, and we heard that you had a near fatal confrontation with Mr Ormond's prize bull. Is that true?'

'It was unhealthy, to say the least,' retorted Amanda, smiling ruefully at the memory of the incident. 'But it really wasn't too bad.'

'But you had tea with Mr Ormond at the farm, didn't you? It's unheard of, really! Even Matron hasn't been invited there.'

'So it was explained to me. I hope the fact that I was won't make life difficult for me,' said Amanda, smiling faintly.

'Don't worry about that. Anyone who can come in here and make Mr Ormond relent is something of a heroine. He's been making our lives a misery, I can tell you. I should think you're more of a snake charmer than a nurse, if you have managed to master him.'

'I don't think that is the situation at all,' responded Amanda, smiling. 'But I gather that Mr Ormond has relented his attitude a little in our favour, and it seems that I have to play along to get him to maintain this new outlook.'

'Anything for a quiet life.' There was just the faintest suspicion of a Scots brogue in Heather Stewart's voice. 'It's bad enough having to live out here, but when most of the footpaths are barred to us then life gets even more difficult. Some of the nurses have left because of the trouble we've had.'

'Was it really as bad as that?' Amanda sounded surprised, for she could not believe that Charles Ormond would act in such a petty manner.

'Well, it's difficult to say, but incidents do tend to blow up out of all perspective. Yet some of the rules they tried to enforce seemed rather old-fashioned, to say the least.'

Richard Ormond appeared in the doorway, and there was a tense expression upon his face. He nodded as Sister Stewart looked at him.

'You're right,' he said slowly. 'I think she's losing ground now. I've decided to try another course of treatment, and have already administered the first dose. Watch her very carefully now, won't you? Call me out if you see the slightest change in her condition.'

Sister Stewart nodded respectfully. 'I do hope she'll be all right. Poor old soul. Her daughter is coming at the end of the week, and Mrs West said that they hadn't seen each other for fifteen years.'

'I think she'll pull through, unless there are complications, so we must maintain the closest observation upon her.' There was a grave note in Richard's tone, and Amanda realized that, as yet, she was not involved in the grim routine of the Hall, but in the morning she would take up her responsibilities, and that was a sobering thought as she followed Richard from the office. He paused at the foot of the stairs.

'It must have been quite a full day for you,' he commented, smiling faintly as he met her gaze. 'You've certainly been thrown in at the deep end as far as my father is concerned. But that seems to have been all to the good. I hope things will ease slightly now. But I'll see you on duty in the morning, Amanda. Thank you for making my evening off a pleasant one.'

'I enjoyed it,' she responded. 'Thank you for helping me settle in so well.'

She went up to her apartment and retired, lying in her bed for some considerable time before sleep could be induced to visit her, and she considered the events of the day. Now she really was on the threshold of the new life she had promised herself, and all the signs were that her hopes could be fulfilled. As she drifted into slumber she held an image of Richard Ormond's face in her mind, and vowed that she would do all that was within her power to help ease the burden he so obviously carried.

The next thing she knew, a hand was gently shaking her shoulder, and Amanda awakened with a start to find smiling Sister Stewart peering down at her.

'It's six-fifteen, Amanda,' declared the night Sister. 'I always call the morning Sister. Perhaps you'll be in the office at about five to seven, and I'll go over the reports with you.'

'Certainly, and thanks for calling me.' Amanda sat up in bed. 'I usually awaken quite early, but being in strange surroundings, I expect my mental clock hasn't adjusted.'

'Breakfast will be ready for you in the dining room as soon as you wish to have it,' continued Heather Stewart. 'You'll find the rest of your shift there, I expect.' She turned away, pausing at the door. 'I wish you luck in your duties here, and hope you will be as happy as the rest of us.'

'Thank you.' Amanda smiled as she slipped out of bed and reached for her dressing gown. 'I'll see you just before seven.'

She hurriedly prepared for duty, aware that Heather Stewart would now be ready to hand over her responsibilities. She had no intention of being late, and when she had showered and made up and donned her uniform she quietly left her room and went down to the dining room.

There were four nurses present in the room; three of them sitting together at one table and the fourth, a staff nurse, seated by herself. Nurse Fleming, whom Amanda had met the previous morning, arose, smiling, to greet her, and introduced the other two nurses at her table. Nurse Rose Everard was a tall, slim blonde in her middle twenties, with an attractive face, although her lips were set in rather a thin line. But she spoke pleasantly enough, and Amanda turned her attention to Nadine Clayton, who was medium-sized, in her twenties, and obviously a cheerful type, with gleaming brown eyes and short, black wavy hair.

'Pleased to meet you, Sister,' she greeted. 'I hope you'll like working here.'

'That's Staff Nurse Brant,' continued Stacey Fleming, indicating the lone figure at the adjacent table, and Amanda turned to greet the fourth member of her shift.

'Good morning, Nurse,' she said briskly, moving towards the table and smiling her thanks at Nurse Fleming as she departed. 'I shall be relying a great deal upon you this morning to show me the routine.'

'I'm sure you'll settle in quite well,' came the smooth reply, and Amanda gazed more intently at the slim brunette, intrigued more by the tone of the sophisticated voice than anything else. But Thelma Brant's lovely face was impassive, although there was a smile upon her full lips.

'Thank you, I'm sure I will,' replied Amanda, and, as she went to help herself to the breakfast which had been prepared she wondered if there would be friction between herself and Thelma Brant. There had been animosity in the girl's tones, but Amanda refused to permit herself the luxury of pre-judging the situation until she had learned more about all of her staff. She went to Thelma's table, hoping for a chat, but the girl arose and departed before Amanda could sit down.

'Sister, you'll find Thelma a little bit stand-offish,' said Stacey Fleming when the dining room door had closed behind the staff nurse. 'There's a jealous streak in her, and she was rather hoping that she would be promoted to the position you've come to take up. So don't be surprised if she doesn't seem to welcome your arrival. She isn't a friendly type at all, and I believe she has designs upon Doctor Ormond. But what happened to you yesterday? We heard you were almost gored by the bull, and you had trouble with Mr Ormond.'

'There was no trouble, and I did have a rather narrow escape in that bull incident.' Amanda sat down and began to eat her breakfast, aware that time was slipping away, and she had no desire to be late for duty on her first day. She explained some of what had occurred while she ate her meal, and soon realized that she would get along fine with the three nurses. They were pleasant and friendly, and that pleased Amanda because they would be working very closely together. Even Rose Everard joined in the conversation, although she seemed less friendly than the other two. But it was Thelma Brant who worried Amanda, for if there was antipathy between them then it could make all the difference between success and failure for Amanda in this exacting position.

But it was a challenge which she had to

meet, and she vowed silently that she would do all within her power to prove competent and efficient. Nothing could be permitted to spoil the fine start she had made. There was a situation here at the Hall which could stand a great deal of improvement, and it appeared that she was in a position to help. If fate had decided to use her then she could only involve herself as much as possible and do all that she could. Thinking of Richard Ormond, she knew that he needed help, and there was a strange, warm feeling in her breast as she finished her meal.

She was needed here. That was the most important point which made itself evident. After losing her mother and having nothing to hold on to, she had arrived to find that her presence was an asset, and that was all she needed. There was justification for her existence, and she arose to go on duty with a keen eagerness vibrant in her mind.

FOUR

At ten minutes to seven Amanda walked into the duty office on the ground floor to find Sister Stewart at the desk rounding off her reports, and Richard Ormond was seated by the desk, a cup of coffee in his hands. He arose at Amanda's entrance, forcing a smile on his tired face, and she wondered if he had been up all night.

'Good morning, Sister,' he greeted in low tones. 'You're looking quite brisk and efficient.'

'Good morning, Doctor,' she responded. 'How is Mrs West this morning?'

He sighed heavily and sat down again, putting aside his coffee. 'I've been up most of the night with her, but I think we're winning,' he replied heavily. 'She's beginning to respond to the new treatment.

However I'll let you take over here so that Sister Stewart can get off duty. When she's put you in the picture I'll be back to make a round with you.' He arose and walked to the door. 'Thanks for all your help during the night, Sister,' he said to Heather Stewart. 'Sleep well today.'

'Thank you, Doctor,' responded the girl, smiling. 'You try and find the time to get some rest yourself.'

He departed, and Amanda walked around the desk.

'He works for too hard,' continued Heather Stewart as the sound of Richard's feet receded along the corridor. 'I don't think he got more than an hour's sleep all night. But let me get these reports finished, then I can hand over to you. It has been a trying night.'

Amanda remained silent, but there were footsteps in the corridor, and when she peered outside she found her staff arriving to take up their duties. There were four other nurses arriving also, and it was obvious that they were the night staff preparing to go off duty.

'The nurses will hand over among themselves,' said Heather Stewart. 'Your staff nurse will attend to the diets and injections, and she'll show you the ropes until you pick up the routine.'

Amanda nodded, and went over the reports with her colleague. Heather Stewart proved to be an efficient nurse with the whole situation of the nursing home at her fingertips, and she indicated a pad on which she had jotted personal details of most of the patients. She smiled as she explained some of the foibles of their charges, and when she had completed the hand-over, Amanda thanked her warmly for taking so much trouble.

'That's all right. I remember when I first came here. It was a bit more disorganized than it is at the moment. I was thankful for all the information I could get. But don't worry. If I know Doctor Ormond he will be here most of the morning with you. And

Matron will be on hand if there's anything you can't handle yourself.'

'Thanks.' Amanda frowned as she glanced at the clock. 'You're way over your time as it is. I think I can manage now. Go and get your breakfast, then turn in, and have a good sleep. I'll see you later.'

Heather Stewart nodded and departed gratefully, and Amanda sighed as she gazed down at the mass of reports and notes. Then she went to the door and looked into the corridor. There were no signs of her staff or the night nurses, and she picked up a complete list of the patients and went resolutely to the door numbered One. It was time to get personally acquainted with the patients.

Having seen most of them the day before, Amanda knew roughly what to expect, and she soon discovered that her staff were well trained and efficient. They had taken over the breakfast round from the night nurses, and were busy feeding the patients. Staff Nurse Brant was already handling the injections list, and when Amanda entered Room Seven and found Thelma Brant administering an injection she paused to watch. Her subordinate completed the treatment, then turned to face her.

'Is there anything I can do for you, Sister?' she demanded, and although she was asking if she could help, there was something in her tone which suggested to Amanda that she was interfering and that she wanted no interference in her own sphere of activities.

'No. Please carry on,' replied Amanda. 'I'm making a general round of patients. That is what the Sister is expected to do first, isn't it?'

'That's right. There are thirty-four patients altogether, and when you have checked them all it will be time for you to expect the Doctor and make the round again, filling in details of treatments and opinions. I'll see to it that the nurses do their duties while you assist Doctor Ormond.' There was a slight pause before Thelma Brant continued. 'I was doing that job until you were appointed, Sister.'

'I'm sure you did it very well,' observed Amanda without hesitation. She went on her way, and found Richard Ormond waiting in her office when she finally returned to it, her head reeling slightly from all the mental notes she had made and the mass of detail she had collected.

'Hello,' he greeted wearily. He had shaved, Amanda noted, and looked slightly less harassed, but there were lines on his face and his eyes showed tiredness. 'How are you getting along?'

'Fine, thank you,' she replied, smiling. 'It's fortunate that you have such an efficient staff. They don't need supervising. Are you ready to make your round now?'

'Not just yet. I assume you've just completed yours.'

'Yes, and everything is all right as far as I can tell. Mrs West is still holding her own, according to the chart.'

'I was worried about her during the night, and at one stage I thought I was losing the battle. But we have her steady once more. She is not to be disturbed, and must have no visitors today. If anyone does turn up to see her then they must be referred to me.'

'I'll make a note of that. I shan't be on duty later.' Amanda took up a pad and scribbled a note.

'What are your plans for later in the day?' he asked.

'I haven't made any. I'll think about that at three, when I go off duty.'

'I've just had breakfast with my father, and he expects to see you this afternoon. I'm supposed to give you a riding lesson.'

'I don't mind for myself, because I don't have any plans, but surely you should get some rest when you can, Doctor!'

'I'll make up my sleep here and there. A cat-nap works wonders, you know.'

'But they can't take the place of a real sleep for long,' she admonished severely, and saw him smile.

'I'll sleep early this evening, and, with any luck, I won't be called out tonight, if we can keep Mrs West settled. She's the only patient causing me concern at the moment. But, no doubt, you have noticed that the majority of our patients are rather old, and they are never the same two days running.'

'Yes, so I've noticed, and I've made some notes of my own, although Sister Stewart's notes are comprehensive. There are at least seven patients I want to keep an extra close eye on.'

'I could probably list them for you,' he retorted, smiling. 'It's a relief to know that I have found another very efficient Sister. In another week you'll be able to run this place single-handed.'

'Now that is an over-statement,' countered Amanda.

A buzzer sounded, and she glanced up at the indicator board, to see Number Fifteen flashing.

'That will be Mrs Sampson,' said Richard. 'I'm afraid that you are going to find several of the patients a nuisance. As in a hospital, you get a minority who think you have nothing else to do all day but run around for them.'

'I'll soon get to know them,' responded Amanda, 'but they ring probably because they're lonely, and they don't think that someone else might be in real need.'

'You sound as if you're dedicated to your job,' he commented, following her as she left the office. 'If you answer that indicator board immediately someone rings, you're going to be worn out by the time your shift comes to an end.'

'One must always answer promptly,' she retorted firmly. 'It's quite possible that an emergency is developing.'

He nodded, and accompanied her to Number Fifteen. Amanda opened the door and entered the room to find the woman patient slumped over sideways in the bed, and Richard ran past her and quickly examined the woman. He looked up, relief showing in his face.

'It's all right,' he announced. 'She is prone to these attacks. They are based in the emotional problems she's experiencing, and I'm arranging for her to be visited by a psychiatrist. There's nothing that we can do to alleviate her situation by nursing.'

The woman began to moan, and slowly regained her consciousness. When she saw Richard Ormond she showed great relief.

'I only just managed to ring the bell before I passed out,' she explained.

'You had a warning that something was about to happen this time?' he demanded. 'On other occasions you've told me that it happened unexpectedly.'

'That's right, but this time it felt just like a fainting fit. I heard a buzzing in my ears, and began to feel dizzy.'

'And how do you feel now?'

'I have a headache.'

'Sister will give you some aspirin. Just lie quiet now, Mrs Sampson, and don't hesitate to ring again if you feel unwell. You are not to think that you're causing too much trouble to the nurses. We are all here to help you, and we understand.'

The woman nodded and relaxed, and when Amanda followed Richard out to the corridor he glanced at her.

'Part of her trouble is that she feels insecure. Her husband left her, and she has to constantly reassure herself that she is wanted, that people will come to her if she summons them. Her father is a close friend of my father. That's why she's here with us. But she needs a psychiatrist to help her. In the meantime we must do what we can to alleviate her anxiety.'

'I'll get some aspirin for her,' responded Amanda.

'I'll check with you later,' he said. 'I have to go into town now. I'll be back in an hour. Then we can make my round. Just watch Mrs West very closely, won't you?'

'Certainly. Shall I be able to contact you if I should need you urgently?'

'Yes. I'm going to the general hospital in Frampton, and if you can't reach me there then I'll either be going there or coming back here from there.' He smiled, showing the dimple in his cheek. 'My movements are noted almost every hour of the day,' he added. 'If I took any time off at all I would have to inform the duty shift where I intended going. But if you are in doubt about anything at all then call Mrs Duncan. She will be coming round very shortly in any case. I don't think she will stop you in your duties. She usually makes a round of her own.'

Amanda nodded, and they parted; she to return to the office and he walking quickly towards the door. She took some aspirin back to Mrs Sampson, who seemed completely recovered from her fainting fit. The woman was in her early thirties, with a pallid face and rather mournful brown eyes. There was little animation in her features, and even her voice seemed lifeless.

'You're the new Sister,' she remarked after taking the aspirin with the aid of some water. 'What do you think of the Hall?'

'I like it very much. You're a local person, aren't you?'

'So they've been telling you about me!'

'Only because it is part of my job to know something about the patients in my care.'

'What have they told you – that I'm going out of my mind?' A note of hysteria crept into the low-pitched voice.

'Not at all! What on earth gave you that idea?' Amanda spoke in practical, matter-of-fact tones.

'I know what they think. Because my husband ran away with a younger girl! They think I can't face up to life any longer. My parents had me put in here.'

'I doubt if you were put in here exactly the way your tone suggests,' responded Amanda. 'You're not medically ill that you can be placed in a general hospital. This is a nursing home, and that's all. We are nursing you because you have undergone a traumatic experience which has affected you emotionally. The treatment which is being planned for you will put matters right and then you'll be able to pick up the pieces of your life once more.'

'I shan't ever be able to leave here!' There was a plaintive note in Mrs Sampson's voice.

'You're not the first woman who has had to face up to the fact that her husband deserted her.' Amanda kept her tone gentle. 'It happens to a great many women, and they all come to terms with it eventually.'

'You don't know what it's like. Unless you've experienced it you can't possibly imagine what it feels like.'

'Just lie back and rest. That's all you need right now. If you don't brood upon it then you'll help yourself. You are the only person who can help you. There's nothing we can do until you accept the facts.'

'Have you ever been in love?' demanded Mrs Sampson.

'I thought I was once.' Amanda spoke firmly, but her voice quivered slightly.

'What happened?'

'We drifted apart. There was an understanding, but we both realized that it wouldn't work. I sometimes think back and wonder what might have happened if we hadn't parted at that particular moment in time. But you're wrong when you say that we don't understand, Mrs Sampson. We certainly do, and we're here to give you every help.'

'Good morning, Sister!' Matron's cool tones spoke from the doorway, and Amanda turned quickly.

'Good morning, Matron,' she replied.

'And how is Mrs Sampson this morning?'

'She's doing very well.' Amanda automatically straightened the bed covers. 'She's going to rest now.'

Mrs Duncan moved back into the corridor and Amanda followed her, closing the door gently.

'You've certainly got a way with you as far as Mrs Sampson is concerned. She was actually listening to what you were saying. It's the first time I've seen any interest in her manner since she's been here. How are you getting along, Sister?'

'Fine thank you, Matron. I believe I have

everything under control.'

'I'm sure you have, and I've also heard about the way you have apparently tamed Mr Ormond. Perhaps I ought to have warned you about him yesterday. But there are certain things a newcomer has to find out for herself, and I wanted to see how you coped with that particular situation. I must compliment you on getting Doctor Ormond to leave the Hall for the evening. It's the first time he's been out for quite a while.'

'On the face of it I appear to have done quite a number of things in my first twenty-four hours,' responded Amanda.

'All of them the right things.' Mrs Duncan smiled and nodded. 'You have a certain quality about you, Sister. I have no way of knowing, but I do have a feeling that your presence here will have quite a powerful effect upon a number of us, unless I am greatly mistaken. You have been invited to the farm again, I understand. Will you accept that invitation?'

'I have been asked to do so, in the name of

duty,' said Amanda. 'I don't quite know what to make of it, but I assume that anything which will heal the breach which is apparent between Doctor Ormond and his father is to our advantage.'

'Most certainly. We would look upon it as a great favour if you could effect some sort of an armistice between the nursing staff and Mr Ormond.' Matron smiled. 'But enough of the possibilities. I know you have quite a lot to attend to, and this is your first morning. I'll make my own round of the patients, and perhaps we can talk later.'

'Thank you, Matron.' Amanda smiled and went back to her office.

She discovered, as the morning passed, that generally her duties were the same as that of a ward sister in a general hospital, although there was not so much bustle. The nurses seemed very well trained, and needed no supervision. The only note of disquiet which struck through Amanda's mind was when she came into contact with Thelma Brant. The staff nurse had an obvious coolness of manner, and by mid-morning, when the nurses were beginning to take it in turn to have a break, Amanda had reached the stage where she was tempted to confront her subordinate and ask if there was something wrong. But she assumed that jealousy was lurking in the mind of the girl, and any confrontation would only serve to worsen a growing situation.

Amanda was the last to go for a break, and only when Thelma Brant returned from the dining room did she consent to hand over and depart. She sighed heavily with relief as she sat down in the dining room, and her slender shoulders slumped a little as she felt relief from the heavy burden of responsibility which had befallen her the moment she took over from the night Sister. But her mind still buzzed with details and items of information about the patients, and she wrote several notes on the small pad she carried, afraid that she would forget what might turn out to be major points.

When she returned to the office she found Richard Ormond there, chatting to Thelma, who arose at Amanda's entrance and reported that everything was well.

'I hope I haven't kept you waiting, Doctor,' said Amanda as Thelma departed.

'Certainly not. I've only just walked back into the Hall. I will make my round now, but you don't have to interrupt a well-earned break on my account.'

'I can't imagine a doctor in a hospital talking like that,' observed Amanda, and saw him smile.

'I believe in treating my staff as if they are completely responsible people,' he retorted.

'That's the difference between a hospital and a nursing home,' she remarked as they left the office, and together they made a round of the patients.

Amanda had the opportunity then of watching him in action, and noted how the patients greeted him with affection. He was painstaking, never too much in a hurry that he could not listen to even the most minor complaint, and his manner was sympathetic and understanding. By the time they had completed the round she had gained even more respect for him, and he thanked her for her assistance when they paused outside the duty office.

'I don't know if I shall be able to find time today to give you that riding lesson my father forced upon you,' he said as he prepared to depart.

'There's no immediate hurry,' she responded quickly.

'That's where you're wrong. You don't know my father like I do. He'll be watching like a hawk now, and if nothing comes of his suggestion he'll blame me and there will be more trouble.'

'I hope not. I'll go across to the farm this afternoon, but I am half afraid that he may have changed his mood since yesterday. Is he very changeable?'

'No. That's one thing he cannot be accused of. He's taken a certain attitude against me and hasn't relented in two years.'

He smiled ruefully. 'I saw him earlier, and he asked me to remind you to go across to the farm if you had nothing better to do this afternoon.'

'I'll go across and make my presence known, for the good of the nursing home,' she said.

'Thank you. It's very important to me. I know it is asking a lot, and I'll try to make it up to you in some way. But if my father's attitude towards the nursing home can be changed then I'll do anything I can to bring it about.'

'Don't worry. I work here now, and the future of the Hall is as important to me as it is to you.'

'I'm glad you are the person you are.' His smile produced the dimple in his cheek. 'I always reserve judgement on new members of the staff until I've got to know them better, but I think I can safely say that I did the right thing when I engaged you. I do hope you're going to like this rural setting and will settle down here. It would be a serious loss if you decided at the end of the month to leave us.'

'I don't think that is on the cards,' she replied. 'There's nothing in London for me. I've burned my bridges, as they say, and I'll settle down.'

'Well you've certainly made a good start. I didn't think anyone could sway my father. Keep up the good work, and I may see you across at the farm this afternoon, if I can find the time.'

He departed, and Amanda watched him for a moment before she suppressed a sigh and entered the office to bring her reports up to date. It was several moments later when she was interrupted by Thelma Brant. The staff nurse came into the office and coughed loudly to attract Amanda's attention. When Amanda looked up she saw a harsh expression upon her subordinate's face.

'Yes, Nurse?' she asked quietly.

'It's time for the nurses to begin taking their lunch break, Sister. It's Nurse Everard's turn to go first today.'

'That's all right. See that the routine is followed. Just let me know where the nurses are if they leave the duty area, and keep me informed of any changes that are necessary or crop up.'

'Yes, Sister.' Thelma's dark eyes gleamed as she turned to depart, and there was something in her tone which grated against Amanda's sense of well-being. It was in her to call the girl back and have a chat with her, but she fought against the impulse, aware that she might be committing an error of judgement. She had no wish to make an enemy here, and Thelma Brant seemed to be the type to hold a grudge if the opportunity was given.

As the girl's footsteps receded along the passage Amanda sighed and returned to her paperwork. When the buzzer sounded she glanced up at the indicator board, and saw that Mrs Sampson was ringing again. Putting down her pen, she left the office immediately and went along to the woman's room. But this time there was no problem. Mrs Sampson was sitting up in bed, a magazine open before her, and she smiled uncertainly at Amanda.

'I'm sorry to trouble you, Sister, for I know you must be busy and this is your first morning on duty. But I would like to talk to you. I think I can talk to you. None of the other nurses want to listen. They seem to think that I'm more trouble than I'm worth.'

'I shouldn't think that is their attitude,' responded Amanda without hesitation, 'and you're certainly not causing me any trouble. I was about to look in on you again when your bell rang. What can I do for you?'

'I'm afraid that I might do something stupid. It's been in my mind for a long time, niggling away. But I don't want to do it. I don't care about what's happened, but it's sticking in my thoughts and I can't overcome it. Help me, Sister, before I kill myself.'

Amanda caught her breath as she looked

down into the taut face, and she could see the conflict that was mirrored in Mrs Sampson's eyes and knew the problems in the woman's mind were very real. But this was the first real test, and she knew that if she failed to meet it properly then a woman's life could really be at stake. She drew a sharp breath and searched her mind for the right words to say, trying to draw upon her long and varied experience to help her through a crisis. This was what a nurse's life was all about.

FIVE

'Mrs Sampson, there's no need to get upset,' Amanda said, going closer to the bed. 'Just tell me what exactly is in your mind and why you can't master it. I'm sure we can sort it out quite easily. It always helps to talk about these things.'

'You won't tell any of the others about it?' came the urgent demand.

'I shall have to make a report to Doctor Ormond, of course.'

'No. Don't do that!' A closed expression came to the woman's face, and Amanda reached out to pat her arm reassuringly.

'I won't if you insist,' she agreed. 'But tell me exactly what is in your mind.'

'There's nothing left for me in life. I have this sense of desolation, and I keep hearing a voice telling me to put an end to the misery. It isn't worth living in this hell. I want to end it all and find peace.'

'That's only your nerves protesting at the shock you've had,' soothed Amanda. 'Believe me, Mrs Sampson, life is precious, and if you could see some of the patients we have in here you might change your ideas drastically.'

'We're so cut off from life. I only see the nurses, and that Nurse Brant is a nasty type. She doesn't like me at all.' A petulant note crept into the woman's voice.

'I'm sure she has only your best interests at heart,' said Amanda. 'None of the nurses would dream of acting against you.'

'I want to go home. When my parents come to visit me I'm going to ask them to take me home.'

'If you feel well enough to go home then I'm sure it will be arranged. It might be the best tonic for you, but only you can decide that. Promise me you won't give in to these thoughts, Mrs Sampson. There's nothing for you to worry about. You are depressed, and these thoughts are a symptom of that depression. But it will pass, I promise you, and then you'll be able to look back on this episode and wonder what all the fuss was about.'

'I hope you're right, but the future seems to be so bleak. I can't look forward to it.'

'Do you have any children?'

'No. I think that was what went wrong with my marriage. I can't have any children, you see.'

'Did you ever consider adopting a child?'

'He wouldn't consider it. He wanted his own children.' Bitterness edged the woman's tones, and Amanda felt a sharp pang of sympathy fill her. She patted Mrs Sampson's shoulder.

'Don't worry too much about it at this stage. Doctor Ormond is arranging for you to see a specialist, and he will soon help you through this bad patch. I must go now, but I shall come back to see you in a short while. If there is anything you want then don't hesitate to call me. Will you promise to do that?'

'Yes. I promise.'

Amanda left the room and went back to the office, to find Matron waiting there, and the buzzer was sounding and three room numbers were lit up.

'Oh dear!' Amanda turned to leave immediately, but Mrs Duncan called to her.

'Just a moment, Sister. I've sent Nurse Fleming to check on two of those calls. Nurse Brant is attending to the third. This sort of thing happens occasionally. You begin go think that every patient in the place wants your attention simultaneously. But the staff can cope. I've come to tell you that Mr Ormond is here and would like to talk to you.'

'Mr Ormond!' Surprise sounded in Amanda's voice. 'But I'm on duty, Matron!'

'And he is Doctor Ormond's father and we have to please him!' A wry smile touched Mrs Duncan's lips.

'I've just left Mrs Sampson, Matron. She called me to tell me that she is feeling suicidal. I had to promise not to impart that information, but obviously Doctor Ormond must be told. I think I have soothed her, but she is going to need special observation.'

'Don't worry too much about Mrs Sampson. She's trying that on because you're new here. When she first began to talk of suicide we stood by night and day and took all the precautions, but she was shamming just to get attention, and now she's trying it on with you.'

'I wouldn't like to take the chance that she

is shamming,' countered Amanda.

'Well I'll go along and have a chat with her while you see Mr Ormond. He's waiting in the hall by the front door.'

'You won't let Mrs Sampson know that I've mentioned this suicide business to you, will you, Matron? If she discovered that I've committed a breach of her confidence she won't talk to me in future, and talking is the best therapy for her right now.'

'Don't worry. I usually make a practice of dropping in upon her several times a day. I also have the feeling that her suicide threats are not completely faked. There could be a grain of truth in what she says, and we cannot afford to take any chances.'

Amanda nodded, relieved by her superior's words, and she left the office and walked along the corridor to the hall, where Charles Ormond was standing by the closed door with Woody at his side and answering questions.

'Ah, Amanda. Good. I wanted to talk to you.' Charles Ormond glanced at the porter. 'That will be all. You may leave us.' He waited until Woody had walked out of earshot before returning his attention to Amanda. 'You know, this is the first time I've entered the Hall since it was turned into a nursing home,' he mused. 'I hope I haven't called at an inconvenient time. Are you busy?'

'We're always busy, Mr Ormond, but you're a very important person around here, so we can afford to find time to spare for you.'

'That's a reprimand, I'm sure,' he retorted, 'and perhaps it is merited. I shouldn't be here, but I wanted to see inside the place, and to tell you that Richard is beginning to respond to the change of atmosphere that I'm creating. You were out with him all last evening, I believe.'

'Yes. He took me into town and I had a most enjoyable evening.'

'Good. He needs more free time. Are you coming across to the farm this afternoon? I want you to press along the lines I outlined yesterday. Richard must get away from this place more often. He'll give you a riding lesson this afternoon if you come.'

'But he was up all night with a patient,' protested Amanda. 'He needs to get some sleep.'

'Never you mind about that. He chose to run this place so he has to accept the work load. But I am concerned about him, and I think you are just the kind of person to help him.'

Amanda considered the role she was required to play, with both sides in this situation wanting her to act, and she could have been amused by it if so much did not depend upon her doing the right thing.

'How have you been getting along with my son this morning? Has he asked you about your off-duty time this afternoon?'

'Yes. He said that if I came over to the farm he would probably be able to take off some time in order to be in my company. Is that exactly what you want, Mr Ormond?'

'Yes.' For a moment Charles Ormond's

eyes glinted. 'I'll also show great friendship towards you, and we can then slowly let the situation develop into a softening of attitudes. Did my son say anything about you wanting to butter me up?'

'No.' Amanda felt no compunction in telling a white lie. She realized that this situation was so delicate that the slightest error of judgement on her part could throw the whole thing out of perspective and off balance, and if that occurred then the rift would be all the greater. 'He was just pleased to have a good reason for taking off a little time. He has been working rather hard.'

'That's worrying me,' admitted Charles Ormond. 'But don't let him know I said so,' he added swiftly.

'Don't you think it would be a better way to handle this by openly telling your son that you would like to change your mind about the way you've been treating him?' she suggested.

'No!' He shook his head emphatically. 'I never back down to anyone, not even my own son. Let's do this my way or not at all.'

She nodded, glancing at the clock on the wall. 'All right, Mr Ormond, I'll respect your wishes. Now I must get back to duty. We are busy.'

'Certainly. I'm sorry I had to come over and disturb you. I would like to look over the place though.'

'I expect Matron would be only too happy to show you around. She was in my office. I'll tell her, if you wish.'

'I'd prefer you to show me around.'

'I'm not really qualified, for I hardly know the way around myself,' retorted Amanda, smiling.

'All right. You get off duty at three, don't you?' He paused while she nodded. 'Then may I expect you over at the farm at about four? We'll have tea together, and by then Richard should be showing up.'

'I'll come as soon as I can,' she promised, and went back to the office.

'What kind of a mood is he in?' asked Mrs Duncan.

'Quite pleasant,' responded Amanda. 'He'd like to look over the Hall now he's here. I suggested that you might be pleased to accompany him.'

'I'll go and talk to him, although I find him the most perverse and irritating man I've ever met,' came the firm reply.

Amanda chuckled as Matron departed, then applied herself to her work. She went for her lunch break when Thelma returned, and then went back on duty for the final stage of her shift. At five minutes to three she was relieved by Sister Walters, and felt tired as she went up to her room to change out of her uniform.

A shower refreshed her immensely, and she stood under the jets of water with her eyes closed, relishing the thudding of the surging liquid over her aching flesh. Wrapped in a dressing gown, she returned to her room and sat before the dressing table mirror, putting her hair in order. When she had changed into a skirt and blouse she carried her cardigan and left the Hall, following the footpath that led across to the farm, and a taut smile touched her lips when she saw the burly figure of Charles Ormond standing by a stile.

'Hello, Amanda,' he greeted, as if they were old friends, and she could not help thinking of their meeting the day before, when he had flayed her with his tongue. But he wanted her help, and that changed his attitude considerably. 'Not feeling too tired after your shift, are you?'

'No. I'm accustomed to working eight hours at a stretch in a busy hospital. But I am tired. However there's nothing like the fresh air of the country-side to blow away the cobwebs. Isn't the weather beautiful?'

'We could do with some rain,' he retorted. 'I'm speaking as a farmer, naturally.'

'Farmers always seem to be wanting rain,' she commented.

'Not at harvest time,' he rejoined.

'It's a pity we can't order the weather we require.' Amanda climbed over the stile and they began to walk towards the farm. 'Is

Doctor Ormond at the Hall or the farm?'

'He came to the farm about three hours ago and went to his room. I expect he's taking a nap. I'm used to him sleeping at odd times. But then he works through the night sometimes. But he'll be around later. I was hoping he would give you a lesson in riding, but the clothes you're wearing are not suitable for that particular pursuit. We'll have to see about getting you some riding breeches and a hat. Today you can just try to ease the situation a little if we get together with Richard and begin to talk generally.'

'Are there any special points you'd like me to bring up?' asked Amanda.

She was subjected to a perceptive glance, and smiled at his expression, while he nodded slowly.

'You are a clever girl, Amanda. I think you are just what the doctor ordered for this particular case.'

'Personally I don't see what all the fuss is about,' she responded. 'You don't have to let it appear that you're beaten and want to make it up with your son. You could just apparently mellow and see things his way. I'm sure he must have gone out of his way to make it easy for you to do so.'

'He has, and that's what's so infuriating about the whole thing.'

'You look to me like a man who could be big enough to admit that he had made a mistake,' she commented, and was again subjected to a close scrutiny.

'You don't pull your punches either. I hope you treat my son this way. He needs shaking up a great deal. Since he had that unfortunate love affair he hasn't been the same man.'

'You make out that you're a very hard-hearted man, and yet I realized within ten minutes of meeting you yesterday that you're not hard at all,' said Amanda. 'I wonder just who you are fooling, yourself or the people around you?'

'I've got all the staff at the Hall on the jump!'

'They're only doing a hard job of work to

the best of their ability, and they don't really enter into all this, do they?' she asked.

'Let's go into the house and wake up Richard,' he retorted. 'I think we could have tea together on the lawn. There's hardly any breeze now, and the sun is quite hot.'

Amanda lapsed into silence and they approached the farm house. She saw a flower garden in front of the grey building, noting that it was in an unkempt state, and when Charles Ormond saw the direction of her gaze he cleared his throat.

'My wife used to tend that garden,' he said huskily. 'It has been neglected since she died.'

'I like gardening. Would you permit me to try and get it back into the state it must have been in when your wife was alive?'

'I like to look at it and think that she was the last person to have worked in it.'

'But she worked in it because she wanted it to look well, and I think it would be a better shrine to her memory if it was maintained in the way that she kept it.'

'There's no getting over you, is there?' He glared for a moment, then relented, nodding slowly. 'I think I'd like to see you out here working in that garden,' he mused. 'Don't try to do too much at first, will you? And I'll put one of my workers in there to take care of the hardest work.'

'I'd prefer it if you didn't,' she responded quickly. 'I can take care of it.'

'Do as you please.' He sighed heavily. 'Would you like a drink of lemonade while I see if Richard is awake?'

'Thank you, but if you tell me where the gardening tools are I'll make a start on the garden.'

'That shed over there half hidden by the hedge. All the tools are in there. Are you afraid of mice? There might be some in that shed.'

'I don't think I've ever come into contact with any mice, so I don't know if I'd be afraid or not,' she replied with a smile. 'I'll go across there now and find out.'

'I'll come and watch you working in a few

minutes,' he replied, and went on towards the house.

Amanda went to the shed and cautiously opened the door, but there were no signs of rodents and she helped herself to a spade, a fork, and a hand-fork and trowel, carrying them to the largest flower bed in the spacious garden. She shook her head sadly when she saw the weeds that were easily overwhelming the flowers, and set to work immediately, using the hand-fork to commence battle with a rapacious nature.

She lost herself in what she was doing, and some fifteen minutes passed before she was startled by a shadow falling across her. Glancing up quickly, she saw Richard standing and watching her, holding a tray on which a glass jug of lemonade and two tumblers reposed. Straightening, Amanda pressed a hand to her back and sighed.

'Sorry if I startled you, but I had to watch you at work.' He spoke in gentle tones, his eyes narrowed against the sunlight. 'The last person I saw working there was my mother.'

'So your father explained, and I thought it was such a shame that the garden she must have loved was neglected so. But I'm not accustomed to this type of work, I'm afraid, and I'm beginning to feel it in the lumbar region.'

'And you've done a full shift on duty today,' he remarked, shaking his head. 'I would have thought you'd have been happier just basking in the sunshine.'

'I'm not really a sun-worshipper,' she replied, sighing. 'I like to be doing something. Just lying around doesn't appeal to me. But that lemonade looks inviting.'

'Sorry!' He set down the tray and picked up the jug, filling a glass and handing it to her. 'Father asked me to bring this out to you, and to keep you amused. If you're intent upon doing even more gardening then I'd better roll up my sleeves and help you.'

'I used to like gardening, but only when I used to help my mother,' she informed him. 'I suppose this is in the nature of working off my nostalgia. Doing this has taken me back into the past.'

'But only in your mind, and one should be forward-looking.' His tone was clipped now, and as Amanda sipped her lemonade she studied his intent features. 'I'll join you in a drink,' he continued in more lighter vein, 'although I've done none of the work.'

'You'll get the chance to catch up shortly,' she warned with a chuckle. She continued to watch him, and wondered why his father had invited her here only to disappear and send his son in his place. It pointed to the fact that Charles Ormond wanted them to be together, and Amanda believed that she was now supposed to try and heal the rift that existed between the two.

When she set to work again, crouching over the flower bed, Richard joined her, after removing his jacket and rolling up his sleeves. They worked side by side, silently for some time, their heads almost touching, and she caught a faint tang of after-shave about him. Once, their hands touched, when Amanda found a weed that was too tough for her to uproot, and his strong fingers closed around hers and he leaned back to bring his weight into play. The weed pulled out of the soil and they both almost went sprawling, and ended up chuckling, smiling at each other.

'What do you think of your job now that you have one shift behind you?' he demanded as they resumed working.

'I'm very happy. I like the Hall, and I think the staff are very friendly. I couldn't have found a better position.'

'Good. I'm glad to hear you say that. Matron was talking about you just after lunch, and she says that you're top class. I always had that feeling about you, anyway, from the first moment I met you. I'm happy to see that my first impression is being borne out.'

'Your father dropped in this morning.'

'I know, and it's the first time he's been in the Hall since I turned it into a nursing home.'

'Did Matron report to you the chat I had with Mrs Sampson?'

'About her feeling suicidal?' He nodded as their glances met. 'Yes, and I'm not too happy about it, although she has mentioned this condition before. One of these days she may stop talking about it and take action. But I'm having a specialist see her in a day or so, and it's possible that she will be taken out of our care and placed in a more suitable hospital.'

'Poor woman. She must have been really in love for the desertion to have had such an effect.'

'You've been in love, haven't you?'

'Me?' She was slightly startled by the question and the tone in his voice. 'I don't think so.' She shook her head. 'There was a man once, but we were never more than friends. It didn't bother me when we drifted apart.'

'Then you haven't been in love, so you can't imagine the hell it can play with one's emotions.'

'You sound as if you speak from experience,' she commented with caution.

He smiled thinly, nodding slowly. 'I've had my share of trouble in that respect,' he admitted. 'But one recovers, and life goes on.'

'Except for people like Mrs Sampson.'

'That's right. She needs help, but she will get over it unless she decides to do something idiotic.'

'Is she under special observation?'

'Yes. We're keeping a close watch upon her.' He leaned back and gazed into her face. 'You're going to get as closely involved with the patients as I am,' he accused. 'It isn't a good thing, you know.'

'I know all about the rule that says a nurse should treat patients objectively, but they are human and not mere cases.' Amanda shook her head reflectively. 'I find that the human approach works far better than the clinical one.'

'So do I.' He glanced around. 'Here comes Father. Let's keep the conversation in a low key, shall we?'

'I don't think you have anything to worry about,' she remarked, wanting to ease his fears. 'I think your father is a nice man, and he must eventually come around to your way of thinking.'

'He's never given in on anything,' came the swift, almost bitter retort.

'But he's permitted me to come here, and he's set foot in the Hall again,' she pointed out. 'Next he'll be permitting the rest of the staff to have the run of the place, and Matron will be coming to tea. It's a step in the right direction, isn't it? Don't be impatient with him. He's going to unbend and incline towards you, but you've got to be very careful handling him when he does.'

'Don't I know it!' He nodded and arose, reaching out a hand to her, which Amanda automatically clutched, and he drew her to her feet. 'I think you've done enough work for today,' he reproved. 'Let's go and wash our hands and then relax. I have to go across to the Hall shortly, but I can have the evening free if Mrs West hasn't shown any deterioration in her condition.' He turned to face his father as Charles Ormond approached. 'Just look at this flower bed,' he said cheerfully. 'See how it's beginning to look as if Mother has been at work? Put the tools away while I show Amanda where she can wash her hands, Father, will you?'

'Certainly!' There was a grin on the older man's lips, and he winked as he met Amanda's gaze. 'You two seem to be hitting it off fairly well. At this rate the whole place will be back in good trim.'

Amanda nodded, and felt quite elated as Richard led her across to the house. She had hardly been around more than twenty-four hours, but already she felt at home, and she knew intuitively that this was a place in a million. She could never be unhappy here.

SIX

Tea was a pleasant affair, taken on the lawn at a table which had an umbrella, and Mrs Harmsworth attended them. Charles Ormond was quiet-spoken, obviously making an effort to play down his usually brusque manner, and Richard seemed to blossom under the changed conditions. He smiled more often, and his conversation was lively. Amanda found herself being attracted to him by his voice, looks and manner, and when the meal drew to a close, Charles Ormond excused himself and left them together.

'You're certainly having a marked effect upon him,' commented Richard as his father disappeared into the house. 'I've never known him to be so mellow.'

'Perhaps it's because you're treating him

gentler too,' she observed, and saw him glance quickly at her in much the same way that his father did.

'You're probably right. I suppose Father and I have been like a couple of dogs snapping at each other. But he's always so right and I always do everything wrong, according to him. No one can be right all the time, and we all know it, except Father.'

'But the fact that you're showing him consideration is having an effect upon him, and he's reciprocating. In a few weeks all the trouble will have disappeared.'

'You've worked a miracle,' he said firmly. 'How am I ever going to be able to repay you?'

'I don't need repayment. It's all part of the job; for a nurse cannot tabulate her duties. There are too many things that overlap.'

'Would you like to take a stroll with me? I have to go across to the Hall in an hour, and I may be able to take off a couple of hours later this evening. But I really shouldn't monopolize your time. You're being asked to do more than can reasonably be expected of you as it is.'

'I don't mind. It's all in a day's work, isn't it?' She smiled as their eyes met, and he arose from the table.

'I'll just go and let Mrs Harmsworth know where we're going, in case of an emergency,' he said. 'Give me a couple of minutes.'

She watched him striding towards the house, and leaned back in her seat, aware of the ache in her back which was a legacy from the bout of gardening she had done. But she was well satisfied, and sighed heavily as she considered. The sun was warm upon her face, and the scenery about her was beautiful. A pheasant called, and overhead a meadowlark was trilling in the empty blue vault of the sky. Then she heard a cuckoo call distinctly, and a surge of emotion boiled through her. This was more like it, she thought remotely. It was like living in a dream. The grief she had felt at the death of her mother was already beginning to recede into a manageable burden, and she began to fancy that the move from London was working out exactly as she had hoped.

'A penny for them!' Richard's voice startled her from her thoughts and she looked up at him. He was confronting her, smiling gently, and she realized that she had fallen into a reverie.

'Sorry,' she said gently. 'I was just thinking over the situation. I was thinking that I had done the right thing by coming here. It was a gamble, but it seems to be paying off.'

'Good. I'm glad that you think so. You've certainly helped me, at any rate, and for that I'm going to be eternally grateful. Come along. I feel like stretching my legs. But you must be feeling tired, I shouldn't wonder, after what you've done today.'

He led her along the footpath that took them into the woods, and while she stood on the path he went into the trees, to return within a few moments with some primroses and bluebells, which he handed to her.

'I don't usually pick the flowers,' he

commented, 'but put them in water in your room.'

She sniffed delicately at the faint perfume of the flowers, and smiled as she met his even gaze.

'Thank you. They're beautiful. I had visions that life would be like this out here, but I didn't think that it could come true.'

'You sound as if you're completely satisfied with your lot,' he commented. 'But don't you have any ambitions?'

'I don't know.' She shook her head slowly as they continued to walk beneath the trees. 'Mother dying as she did knocked my self-assurance completely out of focus. I was happy at the hospital where I worked, and I suppose I had the main ambition of every nurse; to become Matron, or Principal Nursing Officer, as she's known now. But when Mother died I realized that life was not static, that things and people changed with each passing day, and I accepted that I might not attain the goals that had seemed so precious a few years ago. I'm content now to do my job and take care of the sick. I don't feel any pressing desire to put the world to rights or climb the ladder to success.'

'That's a strange attitude,' he commented, 'but understandable. I hope you will be happy here, Amanda. I suppose I'm trying to withdraw from reality, if the truth were known. That's why I took on this project, so that I could be remote from the rest of the world and run my life within the sphere of my own influence. Perhaps my father is right when he says that I'm trying to get the best of all possible worlds. But I feel satisfaction in this particular line of work, and was never happy as a cog in the well-oiled wheels of hospital life.'

'There's certainly a difference here,' she asserted, nodding. 'I think you're to be commended for the way you've managed to pull everything together at the Hall.'

'I'm still not satisfied,' he admitted slowly, and now there was a tension in his voice. 'But one cannot have everything in this life. If one attains only part of one's dreams then that's a considerable achievement.'

'What is it you miss most, having gained the ambition of running your own nursing home?'

'I don't miss anything in that respect, but when I think of how I could have had so much more help from certain quarters but made a mistake in my selection of the person to help me, I realize that my judgement must be suspect.'

He fell silent, and Amanda imagined that he was talking about his shattered romance. She wondered about the unknown girl who had walked out of his life, and found herself comparing her character with his own, attempting to relate the two in an attempt to discover if they would prove to be compatible. When she became consciously aware of what she was doing she abruptly forced a change of thought.

'Didn't you miss all of this when you went away from home?' she queried, changing the thread of their conversation.

'I often used to think of it,' he agreed. 'But

everyone has a sneaking regard for youth and childhood, don't they?'

'That depends upon individual circumstances, I suppose. I had a very happy childhood.'

'That's why you're a well-balanced adult. My own childhood was good, but I was afraid of my father. He's always had that manner of his. People never change character, you know, and I think that was why I stood up to him so much when I grew up. But he is really a good sort, and it's painful to me to have to treat him the way I do.'

'Did,' she corrected. 'All that has changed now, remember.'

'Well I hope so!' His tone indicated that he had some doubt, but Amanda would not admit to it. She was aware that Charles Ormond's manner suggested that he, too, wished for a change, and for the better.

'Hadn't we better start back if you're to go to the Hall?' she suggested, and saw him frown as he glanced at his watch.

'Yes. Reality is never far away, is it? But I

hope I won't be delayed long.' He paused as they turned to retrace their steps. 'I'm taking a great deal for granted, aren't I? God knows what you must think of me. I impose upon you the moment you arrive, asking you to do things that are far beyond the usual demands made in your profession, and now I'm assuming that you'll be quite happy to spend most of your free time in my company. I should imagine I'm poor company at that.' He chuckled in a self-deprecating manner.

'I have nothing else to do. I don't fancy wandering around the town on my own, and I assume that the other nurses on my shift have their own circle of friends, and, anyway, they wouldn't want me around off duty as well as on.'

'One does have to try and make a life for oneself,' he admitted. 'I hope you're not going to have any trouble in that respect, because if you become unhappy you'll want to leave.'

'I doubt it, but you could always get

someone else in my place,' she retorted.

'No one who would suit as well,' he declared. 'I know you're right for us, Amanda.'

They both ducked under a low-hanging branch, and for a moment their faces almost touched. She jerked abruptly, fearing that they would bump heads, and almost lost her balance, staggering sideways as she tried to regain her equilibrium. He reached out and grasped her arm, holding her tightly for a moment, and she was swung around to face him.

'Careful,' he warned, still holding her. 'It would be a disaster if you slipped and broke a leg.'

She remained motionless, feeling a strange sensation in her breast as a riot of emotion exploded within. She drew a sharp breath, and her eyes widened as she looked up into his set features.

'I'm all right,' she said unsteadily. 'But you're right. It could be all too easy to fall.'

They walked on and he maintained his hold upon her left elbow. Amanda could feel a tingling in her arm at their contact, and she had a lump in her throat. Something about him attracted her as if he were a magnet and she was made of metal. It was an unusual sensation, for generally she was not attracted to men. Much of her time had been taken up with studying and passing exams, and then the hectic hospital life had kept her attention firmly on duty. She had almost fallen in love once, but that hadn't worked out, and with her mother demanding much of her off-duty hours, there had never been any opportunity to associate with the opposite sex.

They were silent now, emerging from the trees and following the footpath back towards the farm. Richard still held her bare arm at the elbow, and the tingling in the limb sent shivers along Amanda's spine. She began to feel awkward, filled with strange emotions that seemed to choke her and repress the easy attitude she had adopted towards him from the very first. He, too, seemed changed in manner, as if his emotions had received a jolt, and Amanda sighed heavily as he let go of her arm, for his father was approaching them from across the fields.

'That was a pleasant walk,' he commented before Charles Ormond drew into earshot. 'If I have the time later, would you care to let me have the pleasure of your company again?'

'Certainly. If I go back to the Hall I'll only stay in my room and read, and it's such a beautiful evening.'

'That would be a crime on an evening like this. My father will keep you company until I return. If I know him at all then he won't permit you to go back to the Hall just yet.'

'You're wanted, Richard,' called Charles Ormond as he drew closer. 'I came to tell you. One of your patients has taken a turn for the worse. Woody came to the farm with a message and I thought I'd deliver it, because I want to talk to Amanda.'

'I'll be back later, if I can make it,' retorted Richard, and set off almost at a run across the fields towards the distant Hall.

Amanda watched his progress, and Charles Ormond was content to remain silent. She discovered, when she glanced at him, that he was intent upon studying her features, and a smile showed upon his lips when their gazes met.

'So you're getting along very well with Richard,' he said easily.

'Yes. I like him. He's so honest and hard-working. One just can't help being affected by his enthusiasm and goodness.'

'H'm! Well we won't go into that. His goodness in supplying a nursing home has cost me a pretty penny, I can tell you, apart from causing me to be turned out of my own home.'

'But I thought you lived at the farm even before the Hall was turned into a nursing home,' she protested.

'That still doesn't make it right to bring in a lot of strangers. I make an exception in your case, of course, but some of those nurses are criminally negligent in their ignorance of country life.'

'Have you tried to educate them?' she asked.

'I gave instructions to Richard that they should be told what and what not to do. They leave gates open so stock can stray. They litter up footpaths.'

'Are they the only ones who use the footpaths?' she countered.

'No. But country folk who use them don't make a mess.'

'There has to be give and take in the world,' she observed.

'And I've done all the giving so far,' he retorted, his tone brittle. 'I think we ought to change the subject. I could lose my temper if we continue in this vein. Let's forget about the Hall and all that it means. How are you making out with Richard? Has he expressed a hope that this rift between us will be healed?'

'Yes, he has. He's eager to patch it up. But he's afraid of making any move towards that end in case you snap at him and the breach is worsened.'

'So I've acted that badly towards him, have I?' He shook his head, his dark eyes gleaming. 'All right, I'll try and mellow a little. It will take some getting used to. But what about you? I suppose you must think I'm a very selfish man, talking about my problems and my son and getting you to help out. You're new here and you have to settle in. What do you think of your job and the Hall?'

'Everything seems to be going well, thank you. I like the job and the Hall. If the trouble between you and Doctor Ormond disappears then the situation will be perfect.'

'Nothing is perfect in this world, although some people can go a long way to making it appear so.' Again there was a harsh note in his tones, and when Amanda glanced at him she saw a tense expression upon his face and guessed he was thinking of his wife. 'I'm glad you're doing something about the garden,' he continued more gently. 'It was getting to be an eyesore, and I didn't fancy having my men doing anything about it. That would have been sacrilege. But seeing you working out there makes it different, somehow.'

'I'll work on it until it is back to its former tidiness,' she said.

'It's too much for you after a shift in the Hall. But it did me good to see Richard out there helping you. I've never known him to do gardening before. He positively hates it.'

'He needs some exercise,' she responded firmly. 'All those hours of duty at the Hall is not good for him.'

'Well you keep up the good work. You've made a fine start and you'll have to continue in the same way.'

'I have the feeling that there's more behind your request than just the desire to patch up things with your son,' Amanda said thoughtfully.

'I don't follow you.' He held open a small gate for her that gave access to the path leading to the front of the house.

'I think you do, but you'll plead ignor-

'ance,' she persisted.

'What else could I want from you?' he countered. 'You don't think I'm trying to make a match between you and my son, do you? I don't know you. You're a complete stranger here.'

'That's so, but I can't get rid of the feeling that you are up to something. You insisted that I came across this afternoon, but you disappeared almost immediately upon my arrival, leaving me to your son's care. I wouldn't suggest that you'd go so far as to try and select friends for him, but I do think you feel he ought to have friends from amongst the opposite sex, and, believing that, I can accept that you are prepared to use me as a means of getting Doctor Ormond out of the rut he seems to be in.'

'So you've noticed that he's in an emotional rut, have you?'

'Just as you've noticed,' she added, and saw a faint smile touch his lips.

'You're not romantically attached, are you?'

144

'No, but that's beside the point.'

'You object to a mild flirtation with my son?'

'I object to the way we're being thrown together.'

'He's personable, and needs to get away from that business of his much more than he has been doing. He took you out last evening, and I suspect that he'll come back to see you again this evening. I'm quite happy with that arrangement, and it's my price for the concessions I have to make in this situation. I'm going to end my opposition to the nursing home, and this will give Richard more scope for improving the place and enlarging his range of activities.'

'In return for my engagement in your scheme I'll better the lot of the nursing staff as a whole, is that it?'

'Exactly. You are like most of the nursing staff – ready to make a sacrifice for the good of the community. Nurses come into that category. They have to or they wouldn't be nurses in the first place. But you're out of the ordinary. I like you, Amanda. I think you ought to go far. I believe you're just the right person for Richard at this time, and I hope you'll go along with my plan and help him in more than just the obvious way.'

'All in the name of duty,' she said slowly. 'You have your share of nerve, Mr Ormond.'

'But you don't mind, that's the point. I can tell. You like my son and you're ready to help him any way you can, whether I ask you to or not. Isn't that true?'

'I think it is,' she admitted, smiling. 'I think you're even more perceptive than I.'

He took her arm and led her into the house, settling her in the big lounge before going through to the kitchen to inform Mrs Harmsworth that they would like some tea, and Amanda considered what had been said between them while she was alone, her thoughts racing like a mill-stream. Richard Ormond had begun to have some effect upon her, and she knew that it was possible she might become romantically inclined towards him. He needed help, and that fact alone appealed to her maternal instincts. She wanted to help him, and the awareness that they were on the same side seemed to give her a sense of affinity towards him.

Tea with Charles Ormond was another pleasant affair, for he could be a most charming man when he wanted, and Amanda realized that he was deliberately using her for his own ends. She had no idea what he really had in mind, but she sensed that he might have judged her to be the type to help Richard, and he was intent upon throwing them together.

Later, Richard rejoined them, after tea, and he declined to eat when his father suggested it.

'Thanks, but I've eaten at the Hall. No problems now. Mrs West is fluctuating, but it is to be expected because of the change in treatment. I've left word that I can be reached here if needed, so I can't move far from the farm.' There was a note of apology in his tone, and Amanda smiled as she spoke.

'You asked me to go out with you this evening, but I'd enjoy staying here just as much.'

'Spoken like a true martyr,' cut in Charles Ormond. 'I wish I could stay with you, but I have some business to handle in town so I'll have to leave you in Richard's hands, Amanda. I'm sorry, but this customer I'm dealing with is an awkward fellow. I'll have to see him in the Blue Boar after opening time.'

'I'm quite capable of entertaining Amanda,' responded Richard, and Amanda, watching the older man closely, saw a faint smile appear on his lips.

'You see that you do take good care of her,' Charles retorted. 'Amanda, when I see you again you let me know if he's acted the perfect host or not.'

'I'm sure that I'm in good hands,' she said steadily.

'Good. I'll be leaving now.' Charles arose from the table and stood over her. 'It's been most interesting talking to you. I hope you won't get tired of coming across here to brighten my day. Now that I no longer actively run the farm I have a lot of free time, and I can't come to the Hall to talk to you because you are so busy when you are on duty. But I depute the responsibility for your hospitality to Richard, and he'll have to account to me if he fails to do you full justice in the manner I would entertain you.'

'All right, Father, I get the message,' retorted Richard, smiling. 'You can leave Amanda in my hands. If you have too much to drink at the Blue Boar then get a taxi home and leave your car in town.'

'I never drink too much!' Charles Ormond smiled as he departed, and Amanda watched him intently through half-closed eyes.

'You know, he's changed a great deal since your arrival, Amanda,' confided Richard when his father was out of earshot. 'If I didn't know him better I would say that he was trying to inveigle you or me into a situation.'

'What kind of a situation?' she queried,

smiling at him.

'Only he could tell us that!' Richard chuckled lightly. 'I only wish I could read his mind.'

At that moment Amanda was thinking the same thing, but quickly realized that she would have no success, and she had more information at her fingertips. However she was not displeased with the way events were developing, and she knew there was great scope for the future. Looking critically at Richard, she could almost begin to entertain ideas about him, and that was without his father's blessing.

SEVEN

By the end of the evening Amanda was even more certain that she and Richard were destined to become important to each other. He walked her back to the Hall in the twilight, and as the shadows closed in she experienced a sensation of unreality which seemed to change her perspective. She and Richard did not seem like strangers. He had taken root in her mind, and she felt as if she had known him for quite some time. He, too, was apparently under the same spell, for he chatted on as if they had known each other all their lives, telling her of his hopes and fears for the future, begging her to remain on the right side of his father, and taking hold of her arm as they entered the grounds of the Hall and followed the path that led through the kitchen gardens.

They parted at the foot of the staircase, and Amanda went up to her room with her mind reeling under a welter of new impressions and attitudes. When she sat down to reconsider and collect her thoughts she found that a corner of her mind was clinging to an image of Richard, and he had gained a definite foothold there. Looking at her reflection in the mirror, she saw a gleam in her blue eyes, and noted that her cheeks were flushed. She had never felt so animated before, and there was a sense of wellbeing inside her that created a warmth behind her breast bone.

When she tumbled into bed she fell asleep almost immediately, but was restless, and tossed and turned, awakening to the gentle hand of Sister Stewart just after six. When she arose and began to prepare for duty she discovered that during the night a tiny seed of emotion had sprung into life in her mind, and it was regard for Richard. Either she was becoming infatuated with him or falling in love with him.

Going on duty did much to calm the restlessness of her mind, for there was so much to be done, but she found herself cocking an ear to the footsteps in the corridor and turning to look around, hoping to catch a glimpse of him, whenever she heard someone approaching. The morning passed in routine, and she found that she was beginning to find her way around without trouble. But her mind was not completely upon her work for she could not get Richard out of her thoughts.

Several times she had to hurry to Mrs Sampson's room, and the woman began to take her into her confidence, explaining about her broken marriage, and Amanda listened because it was good therapy for the patient. There was no talk of suicide, and by the time she went off duty, Amanda was tired.

But she had another duty to perform, and struggled against the inclination to sink down upon her bed and sleep. She changed and went across to the farm only to learn that Charles Ormond had gone out on business. Richard was at the Hall, so she went to the shed and fetched the tools and did some more gardening. But she had tea with Mrs Harmsworth, in the big kitchen of the farmhouse, and went back to her apartment in the Hall only too ready to tumble into bed.

It was then that time seemed to catch her up in a merry whirl, and life became a round of duty in the Hall and off-duty hours spent at the farm. Sometimes she saw Charles Ormond and sometimes Richard, but the only firm fact that emerged from the first week of her presence was that she was at least greatly attracted to Richard.

Saturday and Sunday looked like being a long, boring stretch of time, and Amanda had settled herself to wandering along around the farm and the footpaths when Richard sought her out. He treated her like an old friend, calling her by name even when they were on duty, and she was hard put to maintain an impassive manner towards him. Her heart seemed to pound at the mere sight of him, her pulses prone to racing when he spoke, and she could only wonder at the interest which showed in his face whenever he approached, although she suspected that it was impersonal. They were bound by an invisible bond – their determination to see that the nursing home became a success, and that event was likely because Richard reported that his father was apparently mellowing at last.

'Amanda, have you made any plans for this week-end?' demanded Richard just before she went off duty on the Friday afternoon at three. He walked into the office and sat down. She was in the process of bringing her reports up to date for Sister Walters to take over, and paused, her pen held tightly between her fingers, a smile upon her lips as she regarded him. The dimple in his cheek had become an object of fascination for her, and she studied it as he awaited her reply to his question.

'I'm sorry, what did you say?' she demanded, suddenly aware that he was watching her intently and could only see that she was staring at him.

'Are we working you too hard?' he countered. 'You put in a long stretch here each day, then go across to the farm and work. I've seen that flower garden my mother used to tend. It's beginning to look a picture. You don't have to go across there when Father is away, you know.'

'I never know when he's going to be away,' she responded.

'Poor Amanda!' He shook his head slowly. 'What have I let you in for? It's too much to expect you to go on like this. But I must admit that since your arrival things have improved tremendously. Father is busy now because he's in the process of taking over a neighbouring farm, but he keeps asking about you. A day doesn't go by without him enquiring after you.'

'I certainly seemed to find a chink in his armour,' she said. 'But, to answer your question, no, I haven't made any plans for the week-end.'

'Are there no relatives anywhere you could visit?'

'You sound as if you want to get rid of me for the week-end,' she countered, smiling, but there was no answering smile upon his lips.

'I'm going to be very busy all week-end, and as this is your first week here I thought you'd want to go to London at least to consult with your relations or friends, just to let them know how you've managed.'

'No. There's no one.' She suppressed a sigh. 'I'll just take things easy around here.'

'If I can get some spare time I'll see you,' he suggested, and she nodded. 'Now I must get on. I've got my case book to bring up to date, and there are two new patients coming this afternoon.'

She nodded, and sat for a moment listening to the sound of his receding foot-steps as he walked along the corridor. A sigh caught in her throat, and she felt a pang in her breast. The knowledge that she was beginning to regard him in a more personal manner was a bit daunting, for he seemed so remote, surrounded as he was by burdens of responsibility. Yet her reaction was only natural because they had been thrown together by force of circumstance, and she was positive that Charles Ormond desired their closer friendship, although his reasons were obscure. She could understand why he wanted her to help alleviate the tension

157

between himself and his son, but why he should interest himself in Richard's personal life was beyond her.

Her thoughts were distracted by Thelma Brant's appearance in the doorway, and Amanda hastily composed her features.

'What is it, Nurse?' she demanded, frowning as she considered the impassive face of her subordinate. Another stark fact which had emerged from her first week of duty was that Staff Nurse Brant did not like her. There was nothing tangible in the girl's manner, but Amanda could sense the hostility, and put it down to jealousy. But she tried to foster friendship between them because she could not afford to have any problems with the staff.

'Mrs Sampson wants to talk to you before you go off duty, Sister,' came the steady reply, and there was an off-beat note in the tone which conveyed to Amanda that she was not liked.

'I'll see her after I've handed over to Sister Walters. Is Mrs Sampson feeling all right?'

'She's not ill, is she?'

'You know what I mean, Nurse. She's in here because of her mental state.'

'Some people will linger on in that frame of mind. The approach to her problem is all wrong, in my estimation. What she needs is a sharp shock to bring her back to her senses.'

'Have you ever been in love, Nurse?' countered Amanda in firm tones.

'Yes, Sister. I am in love. But that has nothing to do with my work here.'

'It should help you to understand Mrs Sampson's condition.'

'She doesn't need sympathy, but then my opinion is of little value here.'

'You're an experienced, qualified nurse, so your opinion is valued. But I find your attitude a little bit disturbing, Nurse.'

'Why? Because I haven't fallen over myself to welcome you as everyone else seems to have done?'

'I don't see why you should be jealous of me,' said Amanda in gentle tones. 'You're not petty-minded.'

'Who says I'm jealous of you?' Thelma Brant shook her head, her brown eyes glinting. 'You haven't been listening to the other nurses, have you? I couldn't care less about the Sister's job. But I have heard the others say that I was after it. I'm not qualified for it, so I'm sure I don't care about it.'

'Then what is on your mind? I have noticed a certain coolness in your manner towards me from the very start. Now that we are talking honestly I think we should bring this out into the open, Nurse. There's no sense making each other's life a misery when it could be so happy.'

'I don't know what you're talking about, Sister. I certainly haven't any particular attitude towards you. I do my duty as it is expected of me, unless you have any complaints about my work. Have you?'

'None at all. I'm perfectly satisfied with you. But there is something under the surface.'

'That's just your imagination. You've had a lot to do in this first week of yours, what with having to act as the peace-maker between Doctor Ormond and his father. But that's your business, not mine. I'll make a last round and check that everything is ready for the next shift, shall I?'

'Please do.' Amanda frowned as she resumed her work, but she paused again after Nurse Brant had departed, and she knew with a cold, intuitive certainty that the girl was jealous of her. Yet there seemed no logical reason why it should be so – unless Thelma herself was romantically interested in Richard.

The thought sent a pang through Amanda's breast, and she held her breath for a moment, considering that possibility. But it was beyond her comprehension and she shook her head slowly. Thelma had admitted to being in love, but was Richard the object of her emotion? Footsteps sounded in the corridor and she glanced at the clock on the wall, aware that if she did not push aside her personal thoughts she would be late, and she continued with her work.

At five minutes to three Sister Walters entered the office to take over, and Amanda could hear the nurses outside in the corridor.

'Been busy?' demanded her colleague.

'Very.' Amanda smiled and closed the folder. 'But everything is up to date now. I'll hand over to you, then go and talk to Mrs Sampson, if you wouldn't mind.'

'I don't mind. She's a positive nuisance as far as I'm concerned. She gives me more trouble than any six patients. But you seem to be making a great deal of progress with her. See her by all means, if she's happy to talk to you. That's what she needs. Her parents don't seem to have any time for her, and a sympathetic ear is really what she wants.'

Amanda nodded, and they went over the reports and notes. Everything was in order and Sister Walters signed the register.

'Have a nice week-end,' she said, smiling, as Amanda prepared to leave. 'Have you made any plans? I expect you'll be rushing back to London to see your people to let them know how you've got on this week.'

'No. I don't have any people. I'll be staying around here.'

'I'm sorry to hear that. You must have been living a very lonely life.'

'Work helped a great deal.' Amanda smiled as she moved towards the door. 'I'll go and talk to Mrs Sampson.'

She went into the corridor to find her own nurses talking to the relief staff, and she dismissed them. They went cheerfully, happy to be free for the entire week-end, and Amanda was aware of the hard glance which Thelma Brant gave her in departing. But she went along to Number Fifteen, mingling with the afternoon visitors, and tapped at the door before entering. She found Mrs Sampson alone, and was surprised by the doleful expression upon the woman's face.

'You asked to see me,' she said. 'Are you feeling all right, Mrs Sampson?'

'Not really. I'm feeling very depressed. I wish you could keep Nurse Brant away from me. She doesn't help at all. I always feel worse after she's been in here.'

'What is it about her that upsets you?'

'Never mind. You're off duty now, aren't you? I should think you'd want to forget all about this place when you're free. But you can get away from it all, can't you. It's the patients who are stuck in here.'

'Until they're better,' soothed Amanda. 'I'm sorry Nurse Brant seems to upset you. I'll see to it that she doesn't come in here again. You don't have to worry about her, but how does she upset you? Is it anything she says?'

'Sometimes she makes unsympathetic remarks. But that's none of her business, is it? Her job is to take care of the patient's needs.'

'That's right. I'll have a chat with her, so you can forget about her after this. I think you're making progress, anyway. You're much more optimistic than you were when I came on duty on my first day.'

'I suppose you're going home for the week-end, are you?' There was a wistful note in the woman's voice, and Amanda shook her head, explaining her circumstances. 'Oh! So you know what loneliness is! I wondered why you were so sympathetic towards me. You really do care.'

'Of course I care. I wouldn't be a nurse if I didn't. I don't forget all about you the minute I go off duty, Mrs Sampson.'

'That's nice to know. But what are you going to do with yourself this week-end? Won't you be lonely here all day by yourself? I know all the other nurses go off. They can't get away quickly enough.'

'I'll explore the locality, I expect. The weather is fine and warm.'

'Doctor Ormond keeps telling me that I should get up and go out. He thinks it would be the best medicine in the world for me.' There was longing in the woman's voice, and Amanda moistened her lips.

'Haven't your parents offered to take you out?' she demanded.

'I don't want to go with them! Father is always getting at me about the way I've reacted to my problems, and Mother is a worrier. If you'd met them you'd know what I mean.'

'Would you care to go out this week-end, in my company?'

'Oh, I couldn't ask you to tolerate me in the moods I have. It isn't fair on you. After a week's duty in this place you need to get away and forget all about it.'

'Well I'm not going away and I shall find it very lonely on my own. If you're well enough to go out I'd be only too happy to take you, or accompany you, I should say. You're a local person, aren't you? Perhaps you could show me around.'

'Would Doctor Ormond let me go out?'

'I could ask him, if you like.'

'Please do!' A gleam showed in Mrs Sampson's eyes. 'I'd like to go out tomorrow, if you have nothing better to do.'

'Leave it to me!' Amanda nodded. 'I'll see Doctor Ormond now, and let you know immediately what his decision is. But don't build up your hopes in case he feels it might be against your interests.'

'He won't do that. He's been trying to talk me into going out ever since I arrived.'

'All right. I'll see him now.' Amanda smiled as she turned to the door. 'I was wondering how I would get through the week-end. You'll make very good company.'

'Thank you for taking such an interest in me,' replied Mrs Sampson.

Amanda went along the corridor to Richard's room. There were several seats in the corridor outside, and two of them were occupied by visitors waiting to discuss cases. The door opened as Amanda arrived and Richard appeared in the doorway. He looked surprised to see her, and paused in the act of asking one of the visitors into the office.

'Do you wish to see me, Amanda?' he asked.

'Just for a moment, Doctor, if I may.'

'Certainly. Come in.'

She passed him and entered the small office, and he followed and closed the door. When she explained the development with Mrs Sampson his eyes glinted.

'By Heaven, that is good news!' he said firmly. 'She's certainly well enough to go out. She shouldn't be in bed at all but I can't get her up. You've got a way with you, Amanda, and I'm relieved that this development has taken place. I'll give my consent to you taking her out, but I shall have to talk to her parents. There won't be any problem as far as they're concerned, so tell Mrs Sampson that she has my permission, and you can take her out any time you wish over the week-end.'

'I thought about getting her to accompany me along the footpaths,' said Amanda. 'That would be tomorrow. Then, on Sunday, I could take her into town.'

'You may have to be careful in town,' he warned. 'She lived there with her husband,

and there's no telling what her reaction may be when she enters those surroundings where she was happily married. We'll have to proceed very slowly in that respect.'

'I understand. I'll keep her out of the town at first. But I'll go and tell her the good news. She was so keen to get out that I was surprised by her change of attitude.'

'She told me that she liked you and that you were very sympathetic towards her. That's probably made all the difference. Anyway, thank you for taking so much trouble with her.' He smiled. 'I always seem to be thanking you, don't I? Is it possible that you've been here only one week? I seem to feel that we've known each other for ages.'

'Is that a compliment, I wonder?' she retorted with a chuckle, but despite her apparent lightness she found that her heart was thudding as she left the office.

When she returned to Mrs Sampson and explained the result of her talk with the doctor the woman brightened visibly, and

Amanda left her feeling optimistic. As she closed the door of the room she was confronted by a man and a woman.

'How is she, Sister?' the woman demanded.

'You're new here, aren't you?' cut in the man in brusque tones. 'I haven't seen you before.'

'This is my first week here,' explained Amanda. 'Are you the parents of Mrs Sampson?'

'That's right.' The man nodded. 'When is she going to be able to come home to us?'

'We'd better not talk here in case she overhears. Would you mind coming along to the Sister's office with me?'

'Is something wrong?' asked the man. 'If she's taken a turn for the worse then we ought to have been informed.'

'No. Actually she's taken a turn for the better.' Amanda began to walk towards the office and the couple followed her.

'We're Mr and Mrs Aston, Sister,' volunteered the woman. 'You can understand how concerned we are for our daughter.'

'Naturally, and I'm happy to be able to tell you that she seems to be coming out of her depression.'

'You don't believe in that nonsense as well, do you?' demanded Mr Aston, and Amanda subjected him to a searching glance.

'It's not nonsense,' she rebuked in sharp tones. 'Depression is an illness. Perhaps your attitude towards it has communicated to your daughter and confused her.'

'Are you a qualified psychiatrist?' he demanded.

'No, but I understand a great deal, and I've worked with patients such as your daughter.' Amanda paused at the door of the office and looked inside. Sister Walters was not present and she ushered the couple inside, then explained the situation. 'So you see,' she ended. 'This is the first time Mrs Sampson has asked to go out, and it is a good indication that she is turning her thoughts outward again. The doctor agrees that she ought to go out, and I'm prepared to accompany her.'

'May I talk to the doctor?' asked Mr Aston.

'Certainly. You'll find him in his office. There are several people waiting to see him, but you should have no difficulty talking to him.'

'I'll go and see him now.' The man turned immediately to the door, then paused to look at his wife. 'You can go and talk to Margaret while I'm seeing the doctor,' he commanded.

'Yes, Herbert!' Mrs Aston suppressed a sigh and followed him, but paused in the doorway. 'Thank you, Sister,' she said softly, one ear cocked to catch the sound of her husband's receding footsteps. 'My husband is a difficult man at the best of times, but since our daughter's trouble he's steadfastly refused to see anything from her point of view. He doesn't believe that she is really ill.'

'I gathered that much, Mrs Aston, and perhaps that is partly why she has taken this attitude. She needs a lot of sympathy.'

'Which is one thing she won't get from my husband. But if she is allowed out can she come home?'

'I think perhaps that it might be better to keep her in neutral surroundings to begin with,' said Amanda. 'But that will be up to the doctor. She doesn't really need to visit places which have an emotional connection with her past.'

'I understand. But my husband may insist that she comes home if she comes out at all.'

'It would be some time before she's permitted to come out to that extent. At first we could merely see that she took a walk. I fancy that we have to get her out of bed in the first place.'

'That's true. It's so pitiful to see her lying in bed just wishing her life away.'

'Well I suggest that you make no mention at all of what I've told you. It's important to keep the confidence of the patient in these cases, and if she discovers that I've already talked to you she may close her mind to me.'

'I'll tell my husband. Now I'd better go and see Margaret, but I'd like to thank you for taking such an interest in her, Sister. My husband didn't thank you, but then he's a man like that.'

'I expect he has a lot on his mind,' said Amanda. 'But I'm sure your daughter will soon begin to pick up now.'

Sister Walters returned at that moment, and Mrs Aston departed.

'Still hanging around?' demanded her colleague, and Amanda explained what had taken place. 'Well, that's good news, and a sure step in the right direction. You keep it up, Amanda, and you'll get all the tough cases to handle. There are one or two more of them in the Hall.'

'Well I'm going off duty now, and I plan to take a shower and then read a book. I'm not sorry this first week is over.'

'Never mind. They always say that the first week is the worst, and you've got that behind you. I wish my first week had been as auspicious as yours. You've worked wonders all round.'

'Except in one case,' replied Amanda with a rueful smile.

'What's that?' Sister Walters frowned as she looked into Amanda's face.

'Nurse Brant. I seem to have an enemy in her, and I don't know why.'

'Is that all? Well don't worry about her. She's not popular with anyone, and seems to prefer her own company. She was hoping to get the position you filled, so she's jealous of you, and I do believe that she might be in love with Doctor Ormond, although I wouldn't want you to quote me on that. The way you've dropped into his good books, and captured the attention of Charles Ormond, wouldn't have endeared you to her in any way, so it's only natural that she feels envious of you.'

'I see.' Amanda frowned as she took her leave and finally went off duty, her thoughts groping over the facts she had learned. But Sister Walters' words went a long way to explaining Thelma Brant's unfriendly attitude, and Amanda could only wonder if there was any truth in the supposition. Was Thelma in love with Richard? The question led her on to another, which stung her thoughts, for it concerned her own feelings for the handsome doctor. Was she, herself, in love with him? A wry smile touched her lips as she entered her room. Only time could give an answer to that, so she would have to wait and see.

EIGHT

It was almost evening by the time Amanda had showered and changed her clothes, and then she felt too tired to do anything. She did not feel like going across to the farm, and suspected that Charles Ormond would not be there anyway, so she went down to the dining room for tea, and was emerging from it when Richard appeared, apparently looking for her.

'Amanda,' he declared when he saw her. 'I've been looking for you. I need to talk about Mrs Sampson, although you're off duty now. I've already talked to her, and to her parents. Her father was hard to handle. He didn't think that anyone was capable of looking after his daughter but his own family, and when I put it to him that she needed to break all contacts temporarily with her family he wouldn't hear of it. But I've managed to arrange that Mrs Sampson can go out, if she wishes, in your company. Are you too busy right now to talk?'

'I'm not busy at all. I've had tea, and I've got nothing to do.'

'Come and walk on the terrace with me,' he suggested. 'I want you to co-operate very closely with Mrs Sampson, but don't take anything at face value. She may be using you as a means to an end.'

'I don't understand.'

'It's possible that she wants to get out of here, and thinks you're her ticket. Once you get outside the Hall with her she may try to get away from you.'

'Perhaps I should have Woody following at a distance.'

'No. That would make matters even worse.' He opened the front door for her and they walked on to the terrace.

Amanda leaned on the stone wall and glanced around at the flower beds and lawns. She was very conscious of Richard's presence at her side, and when she looked sideways into his face she saw that he was watching her closely.

'Is Mrs Sampson mentally unbalanced at all?' she asked.

'I don't think so, but that is only my opinion. That's why I want her to be examined by a qualified psychiatrist. She has talked suicide on more than one occasion, and she brought up that subject to you. I wouldn't like to take any chances with her. So it is possible that she may try to use you in order to get out of our strict observance. If anything happened while she was out with you then there would be a great deal of trouble.'

'I am a fully qualified nurse,' she reminded.

'Certainly, and you have my complete trust, but I would be doing less than my duty by not pointing out the risks. However I think that we have to go ahead with this if Mrs Sampson is to make any real progress. I'm prepared for you to take her out tomorrow afternoon. For the first time I suggest that you merely walk her along the footpaths. Don't take her into town.'

'That's exactly what I had planned to do,' commented Amanda, and saw him smile.

'You certainly took a great deal of responsibility off my shoulders when you came here,' he remarked. 'Not only are you coping wonderfully well with the patients but you have a made a most favourable impression upon my father. I thought he was impervious to everything, but you have him almost eating out of your hand.'

'That wasn't my impression when I first

met him,' retorted Amanda, recalling the afternoon of her arrival.

'Well he's certainly mellowed, and with any luck I'll be able to get him to help me with some improvements I have in mind. I haven't dared broach that subject to him, but he's looked over the Hall, and at breakfast this morning he mentioned that he noted one or two jobs that needed doing.'

'I'm glad that everything seems to be working out for you,' she said softly. 'This is a noble venture, and you deserve all the help you can get.'

'Anyway, thank you for all your trouble. I'm really in your debt. I think I have an extremely efficient staff here, but you are certainly doing much more than mere duty. Even Matron is very impressed with you.'

'I like to do all I can!' she replied, feeling slightly embarrassed by his praise.

'You believe in giving everything.' He nodded. 'I wouldn't take advantage of that fact, but it is my sad experience that people who do so are open to the more unscrupulous manipulation of less conscientious people.'

'I have been taken for granted on more than one occasion,' Amanda replied, smiling, 'but my faith in human nature has not been damaged in any way. I'll always do the very best I can.'

'Spoken like a true martyr!' He spoke lightly, but there was an intense light in his brown eyes. 'Thank you, Amanda. I'm very happy that you are here with us.'

'It's my pleasure,' she responded, glancing around at her surroundings. 'This is just what the doctor ordered. I love the countryside, and this is the perfect time of the year to see it. I'll take Mrs Sampson up to the ruined abbey tomorrow afternoon. I hope it will be fine.'

'The forecast is that it should be.' He nodded. 'I'd like to be able to find the time to accompany you, but I think it would be better for you to be alone with Mrs Sampson for the first time. It will give her confidence and a sense of companionship if you are alone with her.'

Amanda nodded. 'Don't worry,' she said. 'I'll see that she is treated in the correct manner.'

'Thank you.' He suppressed a sigh and glanced around. 'Well, I'll have to run. It's going to be a busy time for me this week-end. I'll see you after tomorrow afternoon to get a report on Mrs Sampson from you. I should think that she ought to be able to manage to walk to the ruins and back again. That would be far enough for her first outing.'

They parted, and Amanda watched his tall figure with speculation in her eyes as he departed. There was a kind of leaping eagerness inside her, and she felt the urge to want to prove herself in his eyes, although he already appeared to have a high opinion of her standard of nursing. She sighed slowly, ridding herself of an accumulation of emotion, and tried to relax. But there was a sharp sensation in her mind and she feared that she was becoming more than ordinarily attracted to Richard Ormond.

She felt tired, and despite the warm evening she returned to her room to relax. Being responsible for the entire Clinic while on duty placed a heavy burden upon her, and she realized that it would be several weeks before she really slipped into the routine. She spent the evening reading and relaxing, and went to bed early, lying late the next morning, and then she pottered around during the morning, feeling fresher and rested by lunch time.

Early in the afternoon she went down to the Sister's Office on the ground floor and found Matron on duty. Mrs Duncan smiled cheerfully.

'Come to take Mrs Sampson out?' she asked. 'She's been talking about nothing else since I came on duty.'

'Yes. I just wanted to check that she was still in that frame of mind.'

'She wants to go out, and her father has given his permission for you take charge.

He's a hard man, and not very understanding. But he has his daughter's interests at heart and wants to see her better and out of here.'

'Then I'll go along and talk to her.' Amanda moved towards the door, but Mrs Duncan called to her.

'I know Doctor Ormond has spoken to you about the risks involved in this venture,' she said. 'Mrs Sampson might be trying to use you as a means of getting away from us. She has mentioned suicide, as you know, and if she does have that in the back of her mind then she might try to elude you and make for the river. Be on your guard, Sister, and be very careful.'

'Certainly, Matron. That goes without saying. But I don't think Mrs Sampson is the suicidal type. However I won't be taking any chances with her.'

'I'm certain everything will be all right, but there is that chance, and we can't be too careful.'

Amanda nodded and departed, going to

Mrs Sampson's room, and when she entered to find the woman out of bed and dressed in a pink two-piece suit, she was surprised. There was make-up on Mrs Sampson's face, and she seemed enlivened, animated by her anticipation. She smiled at sight of Amanda.

'I've been wondering if you'd changed your mind,' she said. 'I do so want to go out now. I don't know what's come over me, but since you've suggested that you take me out I've felt the urge to attempt to throw off the past.'

'Good. That's the attitude you should have.' Amanda spoke cheerfully, but her gaze was incisive and she tried to peer beneath Mrs Sampson's exterior in an attempt to see the real intention. But there seemed to be nothing ulterior, and Amanda forced herself to recognize that she might have a cunning patient on her hands who would take advantage of a slip of her guard. 'If you're ready then we can go,' she continued easily. 'I don't want to tire you too much, for you've been in bed a long time. But I thought a stroll outside the grounds would give you a completely different perspective and set you up to accept the right attitude.'

'I want you to be a friend,' came the steady reply. 'I wouldn't want to have a patient-nurse relationship with you.'

'Fine. Then don't call me Sister. My name is Amanda.'

'And I'm Margaret!' Mrs Sampson picked up her handbag and moved towards Amanda. 'I feel a bit shaky, but I'm sure it will wear off.' She glanced around the room. 'I never thought I'd see the day when I'd want to get out of here. It had become a refuge and I loved it, being shut away from reality. But life goes on, doesn't it? No matter what we try to do, life goes on.'

'If you can accept that fact then half the battle is won,' responded Amanda. 'But try to put those thoughts out of your mind for this afternoon and just enjoy the sunshine and the country-side. We'll see how you do when we get outside, but if you're up to it I would like to walk out to the ruined abbey. I don't know if you're interested in that sort of thing, but I love history, and although I have been there once I didn't get the opportunity to look around to my complete satisfaction.'

'Fine. I have been out to the ruins, being a local girl, but not for a long time, and I should like to see them again.'

They left the Hall and Amanda led the way through the gardens to the footpath. When they reached the first gate she paused, smiling at the sight of the notice on a post which Charles Ormond had put up warning of the bull's presence in the field. She explained to Margaret Sampson what had happened.

'I've heard about Doctor Ormond's father,' said the woman. 'But I'm not surprised that he's calmed down after meeting you. I've never known anyone to have such a charming and endearing manner as you.' She paused and looked around at the surrounding country-side, taking a deep breath and holding it for a moment. Her eyes sparkled and she seemed filled with joy. To Amanda's critical gaze she seemed to be completely transformed. 'Listen to that sky-lark singing.' She raised a hand to her eyes and peered up into the perfect blue vault of the sky, and Amanda, looking upwards, spotted the tiny black speck of the bird that was singing so joyously.

'I've always wanted to live in the country,' admitted Amanda. 'This is my idea of Heaven.'

'It's not so pleasant in the Winter, but even then, Autumn has its own charm. Can we be real friends, Amanda?'

'We are friends,' responded Amanda, smiling.

'I know that, but I mean even after I leave the Hall.'

'So you're making plans to leave, are you?'

'Yes. I'm not physically ill, and I feel as if the scales have been removed from my eyes. It was all in my mind, and that seems to have experienced a complete reversal in the past few days. I was told that time would heal my particular problem, but I didn't think it would occur so unexpectedly or so rapidly.'

'I think you're well on the way to recovery.' Amanda spoke carefully, selecting her words. 'But when you return home you will come face to face with bleak reality, and you'll have to try and pick up the pieces of your life. It may not be easy, but if you accept the hard facts and learn to live with them then it is possible to succeed. I'm sure you will do it, but you may experience a few doubts on the way. So long as you don't let them set you back then you'll make it without trouble.'

'With your help I shall,' replied the woman with great confidence. 'I don't know what it is about you, but I feel happy in your company. You seem to exude a great deal of comfort. Just knowing you helps.'

'I haven't been told that before,' said Amanda, smiling, 'but I'm happy if I am able to help you. That's what I'm here for.'

'You keep saying that. Is your life so completely taken up with your work? Don't you have any personal life? Most of the nurses go off duty at the week-end, and they can't get away from the place quickly enough. But you're staying here right through the week-end. Don't you have any friends or family?'

Amanda explained her situation as they followed the footpath towards the ruined abbey, and the warm sunshine lulled her mind. She could tell that Margaret Sampson was also exhilarated by the afternoon's outing, but she was not deluded by the woman's manner and maintained a close watch upon her charge.

'I can't understand any man not wanting to snap you up,' remarked Margaret when they had reached the ruins and were sitting upon a grassy bank. 'You're the most uncomplicated and helpful person I've ever known. I would like to have you for a personal friend. When I leave the Hall I'd like to remain in touch with you.'

'I don't see any problems there,' remarked Amanda. 'I'm very much alone, and I get quite a lot of free time.'

'But you're helping Doctor Ormond out, aren't you? I heard some rumour about you getting along well with the doctor's father.'

'Rumours do spread quickly around the Hall.' Amanda smiled. 'But they are correct. I am in a position to help Doctor Ormond with his father. It seems there have been some problems between them and I'm smoothing them out.'

'You can do everything for other people, but nothing seems to get done for you. Are you being taken for granted?'

'No. I don't think so. I look upon it as being all part of my duty. If I can help in any way then I'm happy.'

'The staff are very nice, with the exception of Nurse Brant. I don't know why she became a nurse. She doesn't have the temperament for it. But people like you more than make up for her type.'

'I think she's just a little bit disappointed because she wasn't promoted to Sister when the vacancy which I filled became open,' observed Amanda. 'Don't worry about her, though. I'll see to it that she doesn't attend to you any longer.'

'I think I shall be discharged from the Hall after this week-end. I'm so much better now that I'm facing up to my problems. Doctor Ormond did tell me that there was little anyone could do to help me. I had to take the first step for myself, and I've done that now, thanks to you. I saw your eyes sparkle when I mentioned the doctor's name. Are you interested in him, Amanda?'

'Personally interested, do you mean?' Amanda shook her head slowly as she considered. 'He is a very handsome man, and attractive. I like him. He is such a pleasant type, selfless.'

'Just like you. It struck me as soon as I saw you that he and you are alike. He had an unfortunate romance, and I don't think he's got over it yet. But there has been a sparkle in his eyes since your arrival.'

'Not because of my presence,' asserted Amanda, smiling. 'It's because his problems with his father are being resolved.'

'I wouldn't be too sure of that. Don't be modest, Amanda. You are a very charming and competent person. A man in Doctor Ormond's position needs someone just like you.'

'Are you trying your hand at match-making?' Amanda studied Margaret Sampson's features, saw the animation in the thin features, and realized that she had succeeded in getting the woman to think extrovertly. She played up to the change of mental attitude because it was the only medicine that would help.

'I'd like to see you make a successful match. It's hell being on the receiving end of a romantic disaster.'

'Don't think about that now.'

'Why not?' Margaret Sampson smiled thinly. 'If I can think about it without getting upset then I'm cured, aren't I?'

'That's true, but can you think about it without getting upset?'

'I think I am. I don't feel that bleak sense of despair and hopelessness that gripped me before. They say that the best way to forget a man is to find another. I may even do that when I leave the Hall.'

'Keep thinking along those lines and you'll be out of the wood in no time at all.' Amanda glanced at her watch and sighed regretfully. 'We'd better think of returning for tea,' she observed. 'I think this outing has done you the world of good, and you won't look back now.'

'I want to go home.' Margaret arose and stretched, glancing around as she did so. 'I can't wait now to leave the Hall.'

'Doctor Ormond may wish you to stay a while longer, but the best thing for you is to be back in your own familiar surroundings.' Amanda arose and they began to walk back along the footpath. 'I've enjoyed this walk and chat.'

'May we go into town after tea?'

Amanda glanced sideways at her companion, and felt a slight niggling of doubt arise in her mind as she noted Margaret's impassive expression.

'I don't know if Doctor Ormond would agree to that after the exercise you've had this afternoon. You've spent a considerable time in bed and must take it easy to start with. But I'll have a word with him when we get back, if you wish.'

'I'd like that. We could go into town and I'll take you to my home – my mother's home, that is. My own home was sold up, of course.' There was not even a tremor in Margaret's voice as she spoke, and Amanda again subjected the woman to a searching glance. Margaret glanced at her, smiling. 'Don't worry about me,' she said in steady tones. 'You may think I need more time, but I can assure you that I have recovered from my traumatic experience.'

'I hope you have, for your sake, and the acid test will be your return to those places where you suffered.'

'I think much of my trouble arose from my father's attitude towards me and the situation when it arose. You've met my father, haven't you?'

'Yes.' Amanda nodded. 'His attitude is most unfortunate, so you must not let him upset you when you do go home.'

'Don't worry. I feel impervious to everything now. There has been a change in my mental outlook, and I don't think anything could reverse it now.'

Amanda was thoughtful as they returned along the footpath. Margaret paused several times to pick some wild flowers, and she even put a dandelion in her hair, smiling at Amanda as she did so. She seemed so animated that Amanda began to feel that she could be trusted. Then a loud voice hailed them from a distance, and Charles Ormond appeared, mounted astride a brown horse. He reined in and dismounted, a smile on his face.

'Hello there! I thought I recognized you from a distance.' He glanced enquiringly at

Margaret, and Amanda hastened to introduce them. 'Ah, yes,' he continued. 'I've heard about you, Mrs Sampson. I trust you're feeling much better now.'

'I am, thank you, Mr Ormond. You've also changed for the better recently, I understand.'

Amanda smiled tightly as she met Charles Ormond's gaze and his startled expression. For a moment he seemed angry, but then he nodded and chuckled.

'You're quite right,' he agreed. 'I've been a bit of a tyrant, but Amanda has worked her charm upon me, much in the same way that she has affected you, and everything seems to be lovely. You're making your way back to the Hall, I presume.'

'That's right. It's Margaret's first time out and we mustn't over-do it.'

'I invite you both to come and have tea with me,' he responded. 'I've just concluded a most favourable deal for the neighbouring farm, and I want to celebrate. You can ring the Hall from the farm and explain where you are. What do you say?'

'I should enjoy it,' replied Margaret, before Amanda could speak. 'Would that be all right, do you think?' She gazed at Amanda with steady eyes.

'I should think so.' Amanda nodded. 'But I'll have to call Doctor Ormond and explain what's happening.'

'I'll ride on ahead and tell Mrs Harmsworth to expect two charming guests, and I'll telephone Richard to explain that you will be enjoying my company.' Charles Ormond remounted and cantered along the footpath, and Margaret chuckled as she watched his departure.

'I've heard a great deal about the way he's made life difficult for his son,' she remarked. 'But he doesn't seem to be a bad sort of man, does he? He's had too much of his own way, I should think.'

'That's how he struck me when I first met him, but I've since come to the conclusion that he is intensely proud. He wants to bury the hatchet, but won't lose face in doing so.

That's why I've managed to gain some power in the situation.'

'Did you see how he looked at me when I had that dig at him?' Margaret smiled. 'As I'm a patient I'm permitted to get away with things like that, aren't I?'

'Perhaps,' responded Amanda cautiously. 'But don't push him too far in case he reverts to his former attitude.'

'He won't do that. You've softened him up considerably. I think Doctor Ormond has a lot to thank you for, and I'll remind him of the fact when I see him.'

'Don't be so outspoken,' pleaded Amanda. 'If we're going to be friends then you mustn't make life difficult for me.'

'I think a few outspoken words help to clear the air, and if I think they would help you then I'd not hesitate to open my mouth.'

Amanda smiled as they continued, for Margaret Sampson had certainly changed her mental attitude. They reached the farm, and Charles Ormond confronted them as they paused by the flower garden Amanda had been working on.

'Tea will be ready shortly,' he announced. 'I called Richard at the Hall and informed him you would both be staying, and I made him agree to come across and join us. He tried to plead pressure of work, but I made it quite clear that I expect him to present himself, and the sooner the better.'

'You shouldn't force him to neglect his duties,' reprimanded Amanda. 'He has so much on his mind.'

'Nonsense!' Charles Ormond shook his head in disbelief. 'I think he uses the Hall as an excuse, that's all, and gets away with it because we don't know exactly what it is he has to do. The nursing staff take care of the patients. He merely checks now and again and prescribes medicine. I think he's getting away with murder, and he ought to devote some time to his own personal life.'

Amanda refused to be drawn and would not argue the point, but she sensed that Charles Ormond had an ulterior motive in adopting his present attitude. It had something to do with his son and herself, of that she had no doubt, and she was faintly surprised to discover that her own attitude towards the situation was favourable.

NINE

Tea that evening turned out to be completely out of the ordinary. Richard arrived some minutes after Charles Ormond led them into the house, and he had evidently hurried across from the Hall. After asking Margaret Sampson several questions about herself, he smiled at Amanda and congratulated her upon her competent handling of the patient.

'Come along, Richard,' interrupted the older man, a smile upon his face. 'Your best Sister gives up her own time to help one of your patients and all you can do is compliment her upon the competent way she's handling the business.'

'Margaret and I are not merely nurse and patient,' cut in Amanda.

'We're friends,' added Margaret Sampson. 'I feel perfectly all right now, Doctor, and I'm sure I'm quite ready to go back to my parents' home. I would, too, if it were not for my father. The longer I can keep away from him the better.'

'Is that why you've stayed in your state of shock so long?' asked Richard as he seated himself opposite.

'That could well be. But I think Amanda will be a useful ally against my father. She seems to have tamed your father.'

Amanda forced herself to remain impassive, and saw both men exchange glances. Richard seemed alarmed by Margaret's outspoken manner, but Charles chuckled harshly.

'I like a person who has no qualms about calling a spade a spade,' he observed. 'You bring a breath of fresh air into the house, Mrs Sampson.'

'I've been ill, mentally ill, and that's my excuse for speaking so outrageously,' came the instant reply, and Amanda saw that the woman's eyes were gleaming. 'I think Doctor Ormond is foolish, too.'

'I agree with you there,' commented Charles, chuckling.

'Really, Mrs Sampson?' enquired Richard. 'What gives you that opinion?'

'You're wasting time with such a capable Sister. Amanda may find someone around town who interests her, and you certainly need her at the Hall.'

'I'm sure Sister Wright wouldn't want to leave nursing,' said Richard.

'I'm not talking about her work but her personal life. She may meet someone who will sweep her off her feet. If that happened you'd lose her.'

'There's not much danger of that,' interposed Amanda, wanting to change the subject. 'I have the week-end free, but I haven't really gone off duty.'

'You're stuck with a lame duck like me,'

said Margaret.

'No. I'm helping you, and time doesn't enter into it. If you need my company when I'm supposed to be off duty then I'll stay and be with you.'

'That's what I call dedication.' Charles Ormond spoke firmly in order to dominate the conversation. 'But I feel a change of subject is called for. Let's forget about the Hall and all it stands for. There's too much duty and not enough relaxation. All the staff get their fair share of time off duty, except Richard and you, Amanda. Now you'd better begin to revise your ideas about the business. I want to see the two of you getting out more.'

'I'm trying to arrange my duties so that I do get more free time,' said Richard.

'And when Amanda is off duty,' insisted Charles. 'It's no life for a young woman to have to be on her own after a week of hard work and responsibility. It's up to you to see that Amanda gets some company, Richard.'

'Perhaps she doesn't want my company,'

retorted Richard, glancing at Amanda and winking. 'And if I listen to you, Father, I'll be spending all my time taking out the off-duty nurses. I'd never get anything else done.'

'I'm not interested in any of the other nurses,' responded Charles Ormond in brusque tones. 'Only Amanda.'

'She is the nicest nurse on the staff,' interposed Margaret Sampson.

'I'll have to get you to put that in writing,' cut in Amanda, chuckling, but despite her casual manner she felt aware of a diffidence of manner enveloping her, and fought hard against it. She stifled a sigh and attempted to change the subject, but Charles Ormond came to her rescue, engaging Richard in talk about his latest business venture, explaining how he had made a deal for the neighbouring farm.

'Then perhaps we can talk about taking over more ground at the Hall,' replied Richard. 'I'd like to build a Children's Wing in the grounds, if we could get planning permission, and then I'd add another doctor to the staff. That would give me the opportunity to get off duty instead of being on call twenty-four hours a day.'

'I can't argue against that,' countered Charles Ormond, shaking his head. 'I've been getting at you to take off more time. But we'll talk about it. Enough of business now. We have guests, and we are not being very polite or hospitable in discussing business at the table.'

'Amanda has offered to see me after I leave the Hall,' commented Margaret. 'When will you discharge me, Doctor?'

'I'd like to put you under the care of a psychiatrist,' said Richard. 'If you are well enough to return home now you could see the local chap, at the general hospital in town. We'll see how you are feeling by Monday, and then I'll make an appointment for you to see him. It will probably be next Friday. After he's had a chat with you we'll know what to do about you.'

'You think I'm a bit soft in the head?' A

tight smile showed on Margaret's face.

'Not at all. You've been under a great deal of stress, and it would be better for you to see a specialist before we declare you fit to return to normal circulation. The majority of patients who see a psychiatrist are quite sane. It's a misconception that one has to be mad before one sees a psychiatrist.' He glanced at Amanda. 'I expect we'll get Amanda to take you to the hospital when you have to go.'

'What sort of things will the psychiatrist ask?' A note of anxiety crept into Margaret's tone.

'Don't worry about it. He'll only want to know exactly what went wrong in your marriage, and will probably take you back over it. Of course, it will mean reliving the whole painful episode, but that's the only way to get it out of your system.'

'If it will help me get back to normal then I shan't mind,' said Margaret.

Amanda sighed in relief, and when the meal was ended Richard arose and suggested that they walk back to the Hall.

'Come and see me again, Amanda,' ordered Charles Ormond. 'I'm sorry I've been so busy over the past few days. But now this business of mine is settled then I'll have more time.'

'May I come as well?' demanded Margaret.

'Certainly. If it will help you get out of the Hall and improve your condition then I'll be happy to see you.' There was a smile on Charles Ormond's face, and Amanda, as they departed, wondered exactly what lay in the back of the older man's mind.

'I don't know what to make of father's attitude,' commented Richard, as if reading Amanda's thoughts. They were following the footpath back to the Hall, and Margaret was walking slightly ahead of them. 'He's up to something, I do believe, knowing him as I do. He's acting as if butter wouldn't melt in his mouth, and I'd like to know why. He's never been this amenable before.'

'I think he's trying to throw us together,'

said Amanda, and bit her lip, for she had not meant to put the thought into words. She felt a heat come to her cheeks, and knew she was blushing, aware that Richard was glancing keenly at her.

'That thought did cross my mind,' he said in casual tones. 'I don't know how you feel about that, but I think I prefer to pick my own company. I don't like him interfering, but I daren't go against him for fear that he may change back to the way he was before your arrival.'

'I'm prepared to do anything within reason for a quiet life,' she said in low pitched tones.

'Then we'll see Mrs Sampson safely back to her room and back under the control of the duty Sister, and then perhaps we'll go out for the evening,' he suggested. 'Unless you're tired after your outing this afternoon.'

'No. I'm not too tired.' Amanda tried to maintain an even tone, but she knew her voice quivered slightly.

'You deserve a break, stepping in the way you did to help with Mrs Sampson. She's certainly come to rely upon you.'

'It's all part of the job,' responded Amanda.

'That's what I like about you. You're never off duty, are you.'

'Neither are you.'

'That's different. I own the place. But you're only one of the staff.' He paused. 'I didn't mean it to sound the way it did. What I meant was, you are merely required to perform certain duties, but you're ready to do as much as is necessary.'

'That's what a nurse's life is all about.'

'Not all nurses think that way.'

'Well I do. If there's anything I can do to help, at any time, then you have only to let me know, Doctor.'

'Call me Richard. We are off duty.'

'Sorry. I forgot!'

He reached out and squeezed her arm, and at the moment Mrs Sampson turned to look back at them.

'If you two want to go off on your own I can find my own way back to the Hall,' she said.

'We'll see you in and settled down,' said Richard, smiling.

'Then you'll go out for the evening, won't you?'

'I expect so.' Richard nodded.

'I can sense it,' said Margaret. 'It's showing in Amanda's face. You two are meant for each other, did you know? I think you father senses that, Doctor, and I can certainly see it.'

'Everybody is trying to make something out of nothing,' he retorted. 'Come along, Mrs Sampson. You've done more than enough for one day.'

They entered the Hall, and when Mrs Sampson was returned to her room Amanda went up to her quarters to change. She felt a sense of anticipation as she prepared for the evening, and when she went down to the hall Richard was waiting for her.

'I'd like nothing better than to go for a walk along the footpaths,' he said, his dark eyes filled with admiration as he looked at her. 'But you've been on your feet all week, and out this afternoon. Would you prefer to go for a drive and see something of the country-side?'

'That would be nice,' she agreed. 'I think I have had enough walking for one day.'

'Come along then.' He took her arm and led her to the door, and Amanda felt a tingle along her spine as they walked out into the warm evening air. Richard did not release his hold upon her as they walked to where his car was parked, and she sensed that they were being watched from the Hall. She glanced around as he opened the car door for her, and a thrill of delight tremored through her mind as she considered that in one short week her whole outlook upon life had changed.

'You're looking happy,' she commented as he joined her, sliding into the driver's seat.

'Does that mean that I usually go around

with a long face?' he countered.

'No. But the responsibilities you have certainly bear down upon you.'

'You're most observant.' He nodded as he started the car. 'I shall have to guard my expression in future. Where would you like to go?'

'I'm the stranger here. You take me and show me around.' Her tone was light and casual, but there was a sense of anticipation in her that warned of the importance of this evening. She tried to analyse her feelings towards him, aware that she did feel something which was more than mere regard for a colleague. The fact that she had known him only one week did not seem to make any difference, and she had never been one to wear her heart upon her sleeve. She glanced at him as he drove along the gravelled driveway to the road, and nodded slowly. There was much about him to like, she decided. He was handsome, and now that his features were relaxed he did not look quite so forbidding. But the pressure was off him now and he could afford to relax.

'You've made a tremendous amount of difference to my life, do you know that?' he queried as he drove along a twisting country road.

'I have noticed some of the changes, but they all seem to be for the better. I only hope I can keep up the good work.'

'I'm not talking about the way you've won my father around, although that is little short of a miracle. But you've given me something to hope for, to look forward to. I don't suppose I'm making myself very clear, but that's only natural.' He chuckled softly. 'I don't think I've met anyone quite like you before, Amanda. You have all the qualities necessary in a nurse, and then something extra. I wish I had met you a long time ago. But I'm quite happy that you have turned up in my life now. I want to make the most of the fact.'

'Are you running a temperature?' she asked lightly, glancing at him, and he took his eyes from the road to throw a smiling glance at her.

'I'm not making much sense, am I? But then, I'm off duty now, and I rarely get away from the grindstone. I feel like a youth who is playing truant from school.'

'You've been doing too much,' she reprimanded.

'There was no other way. I'm the only doctor in the place. I can't get a relief. But there was nothing powerful enough around the Hall to make me want to get away for a spell – until you arrived. Now I find that I want to be in your company as often as possible. I think you're going to have a great influence upon my life, Amanda, and I believe that you are aware of the fact. Sometimes two people can sense that they mean something to each other, even in the first moment of meeting. I felt something like that when I first saw you, and could hardly wait for you to arrive after your interview. The way events have shaped since your arrival only strengthens my belief about you. You've tamed my father, and now we're out together.' He shook his head slowly. 'You must think I'm delirious.'

'No,' she cut in. 'I think I understand perfectly.' Her voice was quiet and low pitched, and she heard him catch his breath.

'You, too!' he exclaimed. 'You feel the same way I do, isn't that so?'

'I think so. At least, everything you've said makes sense to me, so if you are running a temperature then I am also.'

'I think my father noticed something from the outset,' he continued. 'That's why he changed his attitude towards me. He was on the outside looking at us, and he saw something. Not even Matron had set foot inside the farmhouse, but your first afternoon here he invited you in, then gave you the run of the place.'

'You're possibly right.' Amanda nodded slowly, thinking back over the times she had spoken with his father. 'He's a very perceptive man, and I think he read something into the situation.'

'You're agreeing with what I say. Does that really mean that you do feel something inside, a kind of twitching of the soul?'

'We're practically strangers,' she countered. 'One does gain impressions. I like what you've done at the Hall, and I admire you intensely for the way you've dedicated yourself to your work.'

'That's not what I'm asking for and you know it.' He slowed the car, and when Amanda glanced at him she saw that he was peering intently ahead. He pulled into a lay-by and switched off the engine. When he turned to her she moistened her lips, aware that her heart was beating faster and her pulses were racing. His dark eyes were gleaming, his expression eager, and she drew a deep breath and held it for a moment. 'I haven't had a moment's peace since you started your duties,' he said with a sigh. 'I've heard tell of love at first sight, and I believe I know what love is. As you know, I once had an unfortunate affair, and I steeled myself against further temptation to stray in that direction. But you came into my life and all my convictions dissipated. For the past week I haven't known whether I've been coming or going. Everywhere I look I see your face in front of me, and when I'm trying to concentrate upon my work your name keeps thrusting itself up to the surface of my mind.'

'You've got a very bad case, Doctor,' said Amanda, trying to speak lightly, but her tone was husky and her throat was dry.

'But is it contagious?' he demanded. 'Have you caught it?'

For a moment there was a tense silence inside the car, and Amanda sensed that this was a moment she would never forget. She studied his features, then nodded slowly, sighing a little as she replied.

'Yes, I think you've described my own emotions completely. I feel exactly the way you do.'

He smiled, then reached out his slender hands, taking her into his arms. The next moment his mouth was pressed firmly against hers, and Amanda closed her eyes and let go of the reserve that occupied her mind. She clung to him, her senses whirling at their contact. The frozen places in her mind seemed to thaw out immediately. The grief she felt because of her mother's death relaxed its inexorable grip upon her, and a flush of joy began to blossom through her breast, spreading outwards in waves of pleasure. Every fibre of her body seemed to come alive. His kiss was like a ghostly hand playing upon the harp of her emotion, and she responded to him instinctively, overwhelmed by the rush of sensations clamouring for recognition.

'Amanda!' His voice was unsteady, husky, his hands gentle. 'I vowed I would never again become involved in romance. It was not for me! But you're an exception to the rule and I just can't think straight while you're around. I don't know if this is a good thing or not, but I'm powerless to do anything about it. If you think it is wrong then you'll have to find the strength to stop it.'

'I don't want to!' She heard her voice and it sounded strange in her ears. 'I'm a fatalist, and I'll take whatever comes my way. If we're meant to find something in life together then it will happen, no matter what we do.'

'I wish I could accept that belief as firmly as you do. But I'm not certain of anything any more.' He drew back a little and looked into her flushed face. 'You're an angel, you know. You do your work with complete dedication, and there's that intangible thing about you which attracts me like a moth to a flame. I can't put a name to it. But it is a wonderful disease.'

He kissed her again and she closed her eyes, sensing that there was magic in the warm evening. There was a clear response inside her which she recognized, and she accepted if for what it was. Fate had brought her to work with him, and she was prepared to acknowledge its superiority over her life. She was merely a speck of animation in the scheme of things, and this was an experience which she could not miss. No matter the outcome, she had to go through with it, and all she could do was hope that disappointment was not waiting for her at the end of it all.

Time lost all meaning as they sat locked in embrace in the car on the lonely road, and reality seemed to fade. Amanda felt that she had entered a dream world where everything assumed a rosy hue. Her emotions were aroused, and the knowledge that she loved Richard was vibrant and plain. When she looked up into his gentle face she saw there was no awkwardness in him, as if he, too, had accepted the fact that they were two of a kind.

'I really don't know what to make of all this,' he said slowly, breaking a silence of many minutes. 'I've never acted like this before. Perhaps it's a form of temporary insanity, but I hope it doesn't wear off.'

Amanda nodded. Words seemed superfluous at that time, and she felt that she was on the same wavelength as Richard. He smiled as he eased her weight against his left arm.

'My instincts have never let me down when they've really been working. I knew you were going to be important to me the minute I set eyes on you. But I didn't think it would come to this. I hope I haven't overwhelmed you, Amanda.'

'And I hope you don't think that I'm just a girl who wears her heart on her sleeve,' she responded. 'I don't usually behave like this. You're special, Richard.'

'We understand each other!' He nodded, looking deeply into her blue eyes. 'What is it that attracts a man to a certain girl, and evokes a response from her. There are two dozen attractive females at the Hall, but none of them gets a second glance from me. Yet the moment I see you things start happening inside me.'

'That's the way it goes,' she said dreamily. 'I'm not going to question anything.'

He sighed and glanced at his watch. 'I'll have to call the Hall to see what's happening,' he commented. 'I ought to have done so before this. I promised Matron I would, just in case, but time seems to have eluded us this evening.'

Amanda glanced around, aware now that dusk was closing in about them, and a pang of disappointment stabbed through her as she considered that this wonderful interlude was about to come to an end. Reality was still there, awaiting their return, and they could not remain at liberty for long at a time. But stolen moments were all the sweeter for that, and she composed herself as he started the car and drove on until they reached a village.

She sat patiently in the car while he went to a phone box, and moments later he returned, shaking his head as he slid behind the wheel.

'I have to return to the Hall,' he said crisply. 'They were waiting for me to telephone. Matron has everything under control, but Mrs Edwards has had a relapse and her condition has deteriorated.'

Amanda nodded silently as he turned the car. Duty beckoned, as always, and they were both ready to answer the call, but now there was much more to life than just duty, and she was keenly aware of the fact. There was a future for both of them, and how it turned out was up to them. It might need some help to materialize, and she was determined to do all in her power to bring it about, for she sensed that this dedicated man was the only one for her. No matter what fate had in store. It was what she wanted, and that seemed more important at that precise moment in time.

TEN

After that week-end, Amanda discovered that routine took over and ruled her life. She quickly swung into the way of life at the Hall and assumed her position without trouble.

Everything seemed to be going too well, she told herself, as she went off duty during mid-week. Richard was most attentive, and already her colleagues were beginning to notice how the situation was developing. But if there was a dark spot upon the horizon then it was Thelma Brant, and the nurse made no attempt to conceal her true feelings where Amanda was concerned. There was nothing tangible to guide Amanda, but she sensed the animosity that was generated in her subordinate, and could not accept that mere jealousy was the motive for Thelma Brant's attitude. There had to be something else, something that was more important to the girl, and, try as she might, Amanda could not discover what it was. She recalled that from their very first meeting Thelma had been hostile, and had hoped that the trouble would cure itself. But Thelma soon dispelled that illusion, and Amanda was in a quandary about her attempts to heal the breach that had developed.

Realizing that to confront the girl would

probably only add fuel to the fire that burned, she sought a solution that would ease matters. But Thelma did not want to take the hand that was extended to her. No matter what Amanda suggested, she was politely snubbed, until she accepted the fact that the matter was well and truly out of her hands. And there was no one she could turn to for advice. If she mentioned the situation to Richard he might take an official line, which was the last thing she wanted, and Thelma would only harden her attitude. But their duties were performed without trouble, and Thelma gave Amanda no cause to complain about anything. In point of fact the whole shift seemed to work with well-oiled efficiency, and Amanda could only compliment her subordinate upon her competence. But Thelma merely smiled cynically and made no comment.

However Amanda spoke firmly to her subordinate on the matter of Margaret Sampson, informing Thelma that she was not to make any contact with the patient.

When Thelma began to remonstrate, Amanda cut in.

'There's no point in querying my decision, Nurse. Mrs Sampson has complained that your attitude towards her, whether real or imagined, aggravates her, so it will be in her interests not to see you. If she requires anything at all then I or one of the other nurses will attend to her.'

'Very well, Sister!' Thelma Brant's dark eyes glittered for a moment, but she controlled her emotions and permitted a smile to touch her lips. 'I admit that I think Mrs Sampson is being treated wrongly, but I'm only a nurse and the Doctor knows best. I'd prefer not to come into contact with her, anyway.'

'Fine. So long as you understand that there's nothing personal in asking you not to attend her in future.'

'She's a troublesome patient. It will be a relief not to have to wait on her when there are others here who are really ill and require attention.'

'We won't discuss the patient's condition. That will be all, Nurse.'

Thelma Brant smiled and departed, and Amanda found herself wondering exactly what lay in her subordinate's mind. But there was nothing she could do, and felt relieved that there had been no scene because of her instructions to Thelma, but she soon discovered that there was a hardening in Thelma's attitude over the next few days, and although Thelma appeared outwardly normal, an intangible hostility began to creep into her manner which Amanda came to recognize.

Generally, however, life became more meaningful, with Margaret Sampson showing greater improvement and Richard wanting to spend more time in Amanda's company. Towards the end of the week Charles Ormond sent a message to Amanda, requesting her to see him when she found the time, and on Thursday afternoon, after finishing duty, she changed and went across to the farm, to find him waiting for her in the garden she had been working to clear.

'Hello, Amanda,' he said cheerfully. 'I've been meditating here for the past hour, and I feel at peace inside for the first time since my wife died. I don't really believe in God as such, although I think there is something, or someone, in control of our lives and the whole pattern of nature. But there are such things as angels, but not in the accepted form with wings and that sort of thing. The angels of this world are people like you. You've come among us and changed lives drastically. I'm a different man, and so is my son. That Mrs Sampson is changing, where Richard's medicine was having no effect upon her.'

'You'll have me blushing in a moment,' responded Amanda with a smile. 'What can I do for you?'

'You think I'm flattering you because I want to ask you a favour?' he demanded.

'No.' She shook her head.

'I want to talk to you about Richard.' He

glanced around the garden. 'I think he's in love with you, and I'm afraid that he may get hurt. I know you wouldn't willingly hurt anyone, but if he is falling in love with you and you are unable to feel the same way about him then he's going to suffer another setback. The last time it happened to him he was most cut up, and is only just getting over it.'

'That's what is wrong with Mrs Sampson. She couldn't accept the fact that the world did not come to an end when her husband left her. But Richard is made of different stuff. He can take that sort of thing in his stride. He's not going to suffer any ill effects.'

'Does that mean that you know he's in love with you?'

'I have a suspicion.' Amanda was not prepared to admit to the true situation which existed between her and Richard. Time was new yet and many things could happen to change the whole complex of life.

'What do you think of him?'

'That would be telling, and I don't think

anything should be put into words. I know you have his best interests at heart, and always have, despite the way you've been treating him. But you can't protect him from life, Mr Ormond. Richard is a fully grown man and he'll stand on his own two feet.'

'I'd hate to see him take another beating, and I'd certainly like to have you as a daughter-in-law.'

'Then I suggest that you don't say or do anything in an attempt to make a match, and let events develop naturally.'

'Then you do have some regard for him!' A gleam showed in Charles Ormond's dark eyes.

'I certainly hold him in the highest regard, but that isn't the same emotion as love.'

'All right, I won't interfere. But I hope things will work out the way I want them to. Now what about some tea? I haven't seen you at all this week.'

'I've been spending my off-duty time with Mrs Sampson.'

'How is she doing now?'

'Very well indeed. I've taken her into town a couple of times, and I think she'll be able to go home after she's seen the psychiatrist. I'm taking her to the general hospital in town tomorrow afternoon. She has an appointment at three.'

'How are you getting into town? You're not going to rely upon the local bus service, are you? I'll drive you in, you know. I have some business to attend to, and perhaps we can have tea together after you leave the hospital.'

'I shall have Mrs Sampson with me, and she may want to visit her parents. I'll accept the offer of a lift into town, but I can't be definite on our plans after that.'

'All right. We can talk about it tomorrow afternoon. I'll pick you up at the Hall around two-fifteen.'

'Thank you.' Amanda smiled. 'Shall I do some gardening now?'

'No. Let's go for a stroll until it is time for tea. I took the liberty of telling Mrs Harmsworth to prepare tea for the both of us.'

'Certainly.' Amanda nodded, and she was not surprised when he took her arm as they walked along the path that led around the big farmhouse.

'If someone had told me a month ago that I would have changed my attitude so drastically I wouldn't have believed them,' he remarked. 'Have you had this effect upon people in the past?'

'Not to my knowledge,' she replied, smiling. 'But I believe that one should do the best one can. Life is short and sometimes not filled with pleasure or even hope. In my job I see a lot of people much less fortunate than me. I think the greatest gift one can have is good health.'

'I'm inclined to agree with you. It is a fact of life that one in good health tends to overlook, and it needs a place like a hospital or the Hall to bring the lesson home. I feel humble now, for the way I've treated Richard, although I wouldn't dare let him see that.'

'Why not? Is you pride so great? Surely that isn't the attitude a father should hold towards his son.'

'Don't make me feel worse than I do already,' he protested. 'I'm trying to make amends.'

'Sorry, but I feel strongly about human attitudes. If people were able to show emotion more freely then there wouldn't be half the heartache that exists in the world.'

'It does me good to listen to you,' he said with a chuckle. 'Poor Richard doesn't stand a chance against you. If he is in love with you and loses you then he'll never get over it. Let him down gently if you have to turn him down, won't you?'

'I think the less said about that subject the better,' she responded.

He nodded as they walked on, and Amanda enjoyed the stroll. Charles Ormond had the countryman's keen eyes, and pointed out nests and flowers that Amanda would have missed. He told her a great deal about the country-side, and she listened intently, for she wanted to learn. When they returned to the farmhouse for tea she was aware that her attitude towards him had changed even more. She could look upon him as being a father-in-law, and he certainly regarded her as being more than a mere nurse at the Hall.

Richard appeared as they sat down to tea, and Amanda felt her breast warm as he glanced at her while speaking to his father. There was an expression upon his face which said more than any words could have conveyed, and she interpreted the gleam in his eyes. He had come home to tea only because he had discovered that she was here, and the knowledge that he wanted to be in her company gave more emphasis to the situation that was growing up around them. Charles Ormond quickly made an excuse to leave them alone, and Amanda wondered if Richard could see through his father's action. But he made no comment when they were alone, and she was thankful, for she believed that events should be permitted to develop normally.

'I asked for you at the Hall, and was told you were seen coming in this direction,' he said quietly. 'Mrs Harmsworth told me over the phone that you were out walking with my father, and promised to call me as soon as she saw you returning. That's how I managed to appear so opportunely. But I can't spend enough time in your company, Amanda.'

'I've been busy with Mrs Sampson, as you know,' she responded. 'I do hope she'll maintain the progress she's been making.'

'She'll be going home for the week-end, without you,' he replied. 'I don't want her to use you as a prop, Amanda. It was fine for her to have you as an initial aid, but the sooner she learns to stand alone the better. I will instruct her parents on how to handle her, and, of course, I shall be having a chat with Doctor Sharpe, the psychiatrist at the hospital, before making any decision about her. However I don't expect any problems with her. She's come through the worst of her experience now, and should go on to make a complete recovery. If she can get out and meet another man then we can forget about her completely.'

'I'm so glad! Last week she was in the depths of despair. But you don't think she is merely putting on a face for our benefit, do you?'

'No. If she had that intention in the first place I think she's forgotten it now. There will be a series of crises, of course, when she'll feel that life isn't worth living. It would have helped if she'd had a family –children of her own. But she will have to find the resolution to overcome the difficulties, and I think she will, thanks to the way you've been handling her.'

'Is there anything I've done since my arrival which has been wrong?' demanded Amanda.

'That's a strange question. What prompted it?' He frowned as he gazed at her.

'Nobody's perfect, and yet I don't seem to have put a foot wrong,' she retorted.

'That's a sign of excellent training.' He smiled. 'It was a great day for all of us when you came to the Hall.'

'I've given up wondering about it – the reasons why I had to come and meet you and experience all that's happening.' There was a firm note in Amanda's voice, and she smiled as she met his gaze. 'I just hope that there is some real meaning behind it.'

'I think there is.' He nodded, his dark eyes bright, and he reached across the table to touch her slender hand. 'You were sent in answer to a prayer, Amanda. I didn't realize it until you arrived, but I've been waiting for someone like you to come along. Now that you're here I'm not going to let you get away.'

'I don't want to go,' she replied.

'Did you notice how my father made himself scarce when I arrived?' he continued, and Amanda nodded. 'I don't know if he is trying his hand at match-making, but he certainly has his share of discretion.'

Amanda made no reply, and chuckled

inwardly because she knew Charles Ormond had decided she was right for Richard and had tried to bring his own influence to bear upon the situation.

'I'll walk you back to the Hall when you're ready to go,' offered Richard when they finished tea, and Amanda nodded.

'I don't know if your father wanted to talk to me, but he's offered to drive us into town tomorrow. I'm taking Mrs Sampson in, remember.'

'Yes. But I was planning to drive you in myself. However it might be better if I didn't. Mrs Sampson might think or feel that we were acting as her gaolers. Let Father drive you if he wants to.'

Amanda led the way out of the house and they stood in the front garden in the warm evening sunlight. The flowers were giving off an exquisite scent. The weather was perfect, with no clouds in the sky. Charles Ormond was seated on a rustic bench under an apple tree, smoking a pipe, and he lifted a lazy hand and waved to them but showed no inclination to share their company. Richard took hold of Amanda's arm and walked her around the garden to the path that led through the yard, and they went into the stable, where the sweet smell of hay mingled with less familiar smells of horses, and Amanda breathed deeply, savouring the fresh impressions. Her mind was keen and vivid, storing up facts for future reference, and she gazed into Richard's face, noting his contentment, the lack of stress in his features. His eyes were steady, his mind composed, and she felt a tingle of excitement unwind inside her as she realized that she was in love with him and that he cared for her.

When he took her gently into his arms she felt overwhelmed by her feelings, and shivered under the power of his kisses. They were both oblivious to their surroundings, and it was not until a voice spoke at their backs that they returned to reality. Amanda glanced around quickly, startled by the interruption, and was shocked to find

Thelma Brant standing in the stable doorway. The girl's face wore an expression of astonishment, which was quickly replaced by confusion.

'Forgive me!' she gasped. 'I didn't know anyone was in here.'

'What are you doing here, Nurse?' demanded Richard in rather sharp tones. 'Am I wanted at the Hall?'

'No, Doctor! I'm off duty. I was told that off-duty staff were welcome to come to the farm and look around, and even ride some of the horses here. I used to be a keen rider before I became a nurse, and as there's nothing else to do I thought I'd take advantage of the offer.'

'Quite!' Richard relaxed a little, and a smile touched his lips. 'Come in, Nurse, and I'll show you which horses are suitable for riding. If you are a competent rider then it's all right, but I wouldn't want any of the staff who have never ridden before to attempt to take out one of these animals.'

'I'm all alone, Doctor,' came the steady

reply, and Amanda, watching silently, saw a flicker of animation in Thelma Brant's face.

Richard selected a chestnut mare and showed Thelma where the tackle was, then turned to Amanda.

'I was ordered to give you riding lessons, but you're not suitably dressed this evening. Perhaps some other time, eh?'

'Perhaps,' Amanda replied cautiously.

'I'm not too keen to ride myself these days. I find my work engaging enough. Come along. Let's go for a walk.' He turned and glanced at Thelma. 'Enjoy yourself, Nurse, and take care of the horse when you bring her back, won't you?'

'Of course, Doctor!' came the firm reply, and Amanda wondered about Thelma's motives as they left the stable.

'She's a very efficient nurse,' remarked Richard as he took hold of Amanda's arm and led her along the footpath that crossed the meadow. The slanting rays of evening sunlight glinted upon a stretch of the river. There were cows grazing and lying in the meadows bordering the stretch of water, and Amanda was enamoured by the rustic view which confronted her.

'I can't fault her at all,' admitted Amanda, and wisely refrained from voicing her thoughts about Thelma Brant's lack of sensitivity for Mrs Sampson.

They walked back towards the Hall, passing through the farm on their way, and Charles Ormond was still seated in the garden. Amanda called good night to him and continued, and he replied with the arrangements they had made earlier.

'I'll pick you up outside the Hall early in the afternoon,' he said. 'Make it about two.'

'Thank you,' responded Amanda, and turned to wave again.

'You two are very thick,' observed Richard with a smile. 'I'm greatly relieved by that fact, I can tell you.'

'Not thick, just good friends,' retorted Amanda...

Next morning, when she reported for duty, she found her morning staff in the corridor outside the office, and Thelma Brant was talking animatedly to Nurse Everard. Nurse Fleming was standing in the doorway of the office, talking to someone inside and out of sight. As Amanda's footsteps sounded, the nurses turned to look at her, and Thelma lapsed into an immediate silence.

'Good morning,' greeted Amanda, and received a reply from the other two nurses. Thelma merely smiled thinly at her. There was a hard light in the girl's dark eyes.

Amanda took over and sent her nurses about their work. She made the customary round of the patients, and when she entered Margaret Sampson's room she found the woman standing at the window, peering out across the fields.

'A penny for them,' said Amanda, startling the woman out of her reverie. 'You're not worried about anything, are you?'

Margaret shook her head, and Amanda peered intently into her face, noting signs of stress. But she said nothing and went forward to place a gentle hand upon the patient's shoulder.

'I'm all right, Amanda. I think I'm getting a bit nervy about my visit to the psychiatrist this afternoon. What will happen?'

'Nothing much. He'll ask some questions, that's all.'

'I don't want to talk about it.'

'You know you'll have to. It's the only way to get it out of your system.'

'Will you stay with me?'

'If you want me to.' Amanda nodded. 'The doctor wouldn't mind. But don't worry about this, please. You've made such good progress over the past week. You're doing all right.'

'Do you think I could go for a walk on my own this morning?'

Amanda did not reply immediately, but subjected the woman to a searching glance. There was no expression in the steady eyes that regarded her.

'I haven't been out alone since the cure started,' continued Margaret. 'I feel that I'm not being completely trusted. But I need to be completely alone for a spell, to be able to think things over for myself.'

'I'll have a word with the doctor when he comes round,' said Amanda doubtfully.

'But you don't think he'll let me go out alone, is that it?'

'We're going to be leaving fairly early this afternoon for town,' countered Amanda. 'Why don't you leave it as it is for now? After you've seen the psychiatrist we'll all have a clearer picture of what should be done for you.'

'You don't trust me! Do you think I've been putting on an act this past week?'

'No, of course not! I know what you're suffering inwardly, Margaret. You have my sympathy, and all the help I can give you.'

'Doctor Ormond says I don't need sympathy. What I really want is understanding.'

Amanda nodded. 'I'll have a talk with Doctor when he arrives. Just remain here for the time being, will you? I must continue my round.'

'I'm not going anywhere!' Margaret turned and sat down on the bed, her gaze directed at the floor.

Amanda started towards the door, but paused and regarded the woman. She suppressed an observation that came to mind, then moistened her lips.

'You haven't been troubled by Nurse Brant again, have you?' she asked quietly.

'What makes you ask that?'

'Just a thought. She has been told to stay away from you.'

'All I know is that you and I won't be friends for much longer.'

'Oh?' Amanda frowned and closed the door again, moving forward until she confronted the patient. 'What's going to come between us?'

'Doctor Ormond! You two are in love, and that puts me out into the cold!'

'But that's nonsense! You've been across to the farm with me. You've heard the doctor's father talking. You know that life goes on regardless of what happens to any individual. In a week or so you won't even want me as a friend. You'll be making your way through life under your own power, finding new friends and diversions.'

'No.' Margaret Sampson shook her head obstinately. 'Someone said that the quickest way to forget one man is to get to know another. Well I've taken that advice, much against my will. I've fallen in love with Doctor Ormond!'

Amanda caught her breath, stifling the gasp that rose to her lips. For a moment she could think of nothing to say, and when Margaret looked up at her, misery showing in her eyes, the situation was completely out of her control.

'You can tell me that I'm imagining it,' continued Margaret, shaking her head. 'Patients do fall in love with doctors, or imagine that they do. But I know the depth of my own emotions, and Doctor Ormond is the only man who can help me out of this.' Her tone rose slightly. 'You dragged me out of my apathy, and I'm repaying you by falling for the man you love.'

Amanda shook her head helplessly, trying desperately to find something to say. But this appeared to be outside the bounds of her duty, and she was staggered by the revelation.

ELEVEN

Margaret Sampson smiled cynically as she gazed up into Amanda's pale face. The woman's eyes were hard, her features set, and Amanda felt a pang stab through her as she realized just how badly the woman had slipped back in her recovery. But before she could speak the door was opened and Nurse Fleming peered in, her face pale.

'Come quickly, Sister!' she gasped. 'Mrs Edmondson! I think she's having a heart attack.'

'I'll come back as soon as I can, Margaret,'

said Amanda, turning to the door. 'Please stay in your room until I return, will you?' She did not wait for a reply but left hurriedly, instructing Nurse Fleming to fetch Doctor Ormond.

Hurrying to Mrs Edmondson's room, Amanda entered to find the woman in bed and apparently lifeless, with Matron bending over her, attempting to revive her. Mrs Duncan was pounding the woman's breast with steady movements, and ignored Amanda while she worked. Amanda turned and left the room, hurrying to the office and using her key to unlock the drugs cabinet. She removed an ampoule and relocked the cabinet, then went along to the sterilizing room to prepare a special syringe, fixing a long needle in place on the barrel, and as she placed the syringe in a kidney dish Richard appeared in the doorway. He was breathless, his face tense.

'Thank you,' he said, noting the syringe and ampoule. 'That's just what I wanted.' He took the ampoule and the syringe and quickly plunged the needle into the ampoule, drawing up the colourless stimulant into the barrel of the instrument. Amanda followed him as he hurried along the corridor to the patient's room, where Mrs Duncan was now holding an oxygen mask over the patient's blue face. Amanda took hold of the patient's shoulders, her gaze intent upon Richard's steady hands. The fingers of his left hand moved lightly over the ribcage, seeking the spot where he wished to make the injection, and Amanda seemed to restrain her breathing as the long needle was eased through the skin and flesh, sinking deep into the chest. The plunger of the syringe was depressed, forcing the fluid from the barrel, and Amanda moved slightly in order to reach the patient's wrist, her sensitive fingers hoping for the leaping of a pulse.

The needle was withdrawn, and Richard took hold of the wrist, nodding slightly as he met Amanda's gaze. She suppressed a sigh and returned her gaze to the patient's face, and they waited in what seemed a vacuum, frozen, with Matron bent over the bed, holding the oxygen mask over the mouth and nose. The faint hissing of the oxygen was the only sound that disturbed the heavy silence. Amanda let her gaze slide to the respiration bag on the cylinder, and her lips pulled into a tight line when she saw that it was limp, with no signs of movement. Seconds ticked by, with nothing to mark their passing, and with them went the life of their patient.

It seemed like a lifetime to Amanda, but in reality it was barely a minute before Richard sighed and shook his head, releasing the frail wrist and looking up at Mrs Duncan. Matron removed the mask from the old lady's face, and Richard reached into his pocket and produced his stethoscope, using it quickly in the hope of detecting some signs of life. But he removed the ear-pieces and straightened his tall figure, shaking his head.

'She's gone, I'm afraid,' he said softly.

'There's nothing more we can do.'

Amanda reached down and drew the sheet over the stiff face of the patient, and she felt empty inside, drained of emotion. The shock of Margaret Sampson's revelation had unbalanced her, and this unexpected emergency added to the turmoil in her mind.

'I'll take care of this, Sister,' said Matron. 'You go on about your duties, please.'

'Thank you!' Amanda moved mechanically to the door, and drew a deep breath as she walked out into the corridor. She paused for a moment, then saw Thelma emerging from Margaret Sampson's room. She went forward quickly, intercepting the girl. 'I thought I told you not to attend Mrs Sampson, Nurse,' she said firmly.

'I looked in your office when I heard the buzzer, but you weren't there. There seemed to be no one else around, so I answered the call. I assume that's why I'm on duty!'

'What did Mrs Sampson want?' Amanda glanced towards the patient's door, and did not feel up to facing her immediately.

'You. But I told her you were busy. How is Mrs Edmondson?'

'She died. We couldn't save her.' Amanda's face stiffened as she spoke. 'I'll see Mrs Sampson shortly. Right now I'd better finish my round.'

'I'll carry on with my duties,' observed Thelma, and turned away instantly.

Amanda gazed after the girl, resenting the tone in Thelma's voice, but she said nothing and continued her interrupted round. It was difficult to put on a cheerful manner, but the other patients had to be attended to, and she went about her duties despite the muddle of emotions that were vibrant inside her. This was the way of life for a nurse. One did all that was possible for each patient, and if a patient died then one merely turned to care for another. There could never be any personal relationship between nurse and patient for that very reason, and she wondered about the personal feelings that had crept into the relationship between her and Margaret Sampson. Perhaps that had been a mistake, although it had helped the patient, and if it was a mistake then that would become all too apparent before long.

The emergency had put Amanda behind in her schedule, and she tried to make up time as she progressed with her round. But most of the patients expected her to stop and exchange a few cheery words with them, and she discovered the usual number of older women who had complaints about the night staff and reports of poor attention. She made notes, for all complaints were looked into, and eventually returned to her office, mentally worn out by her experiences. She found Nurse Everard waiting for her, a worried expression upon her face, and tensed as she awaited the girl's report, expecting further trouble.

'Mrs Sampson has been buzzing continually, Sister, and each time I've been to see her she's asked for you. I told her you were very busy and would see her as soon as possible, but she's working herself up into a

255

fine old state.'

'All right, Nurse. I'll go along and see her now. Just check that Mrs Edmondson's room is empty, and strip the bed and remake it, please.'

'Yes, Sister!' Nurse Everard turned away, and Amanda sat down at her desk to bring her reports up to date. She checked the night sister's reports and compared them with her own, satisfying herself that everything was in order. Then, as the buzzer indicating Mrs Sampson's room began to sound, Richard walked into the office.

'Hello,' he said wearily. 'I just want to thank you for what you did during that emergency. You saved valuable seconds by getting that syringe ready for me. Matron said you looked in on her in Mrs Edmondson's room, saw what she was doing, and went off immediately. That was good thinking.'

'It was the result of good training,' she responded steadily, and glanced at the buzzer board. 'I'd better go and answer that.

It's Mrs Sampson. I was talking to her when I heard about Mrs Edmondson. I think this afternoon's visit to the psychiatrist is worrying her.'

'I'll have a chat with her,' Richard said, turning to the door.

'Perhaps you'd better let me see her first,' cut in Amanda, and he turned to look at her.

'Is something wrong?' he demanded.

Amanda was indecisive. She could not bring herself to tell him exactly what Margaret Sampson had said. The woman might have been talking hysterically when she'd admitted to being in love with him, and to say anything now and put Richard on a wrong course of action might make matters worse. She sighed as she shook her head.

'Not really. I think I can talk her round. Perhaps you'll look in on her a little later.'

'Certainly, if you think so. I rely upon your judgement implicitly. See you later.' He smiled and walked to the door, then paused and turned to face her once more. 'Don't feel too badly about Mrs Edmondson. I was expecting it to happen. We'd done all we possibly could for her. Short of being God, there was nothing we could do to avert the inevitable. We prolonged her life as it was.'

'I know, and I understand.' Amanda followed him to the door, and steeled herself as she walked along to Margaret Sampson's room. When she entered she found the woman standing by the window again, staring out into the open space.

Moving in behind Margaret, Amanda took in the scene that lay outside the window, and saw the river in the distance, glinting in the sunlight. She reached out a hand and placed it upon Margaret's shoulder.

'It's beautiful, isn't it?' she demanded.

'You startled me!' Margaret turned quickly, breathing deeply, for Amanda's entrance had been silent. 'Where have you been? I've been ringing for ages. That Thelma Brant came once, and I told her to get out. Then the other nurses came. Why couldn't you come? You've always done so before.'

'I'm sorry, but you heard the report I got about Mrs Edmondson. It was an emergency, and it put me behind in my schedule. But I'm up to date now, thank goodness.'

'What about Mrs Edmondson?'

'We couldn't save her. She died!'

'Oh!' Margaret's face shadowed, and she clenched her hands. 'I liked her. I'm sorry. I didn't know. You look strained yourself. Does it upset you when a patient dies?'

'Of course it does. We do care, you know.'

'I know, and I'm sorry for the way I spoke to you earlier. It was nerves, I expect. I'm worried about the visit to the psychiatrist this afternoon. I didn't really mean what I said about Doctor Ormond. I didn't know what I was saying, really.'

'That's all right, Margaret. I understand.'

'Do you, I wonder? I know you've been trained and you have experience in all sorts of cases, but do you really understand what a patient feels if you haven't suffered in exactly the same way?'

'We possess an imagination, and it isn't

difficult to guess at a patient's feelings. I haven't been wrong about you so far, have I?'

Margaret smiled. 'I don't know. But the news of Mrs Edmondson's death has shaken me. You have a lot of sick people in here and I'm merely wasting your valuable time. There's nothing physically wrong with me, so I want to go home.'

'I'll talk to Doctor Ormond,' responded Amanda.

'There's no need to. I'm not insane and I haven't been committed. I'm under the impression that I'm free to leave any time I want. Just make the necessary arrangements, please. I want to get out of here.'

'All right. I'll call your parents and inform them of your decision, and tell the doctor. He'll want to talk to you, naturally, before you leave.'

'Just so long as you set the wheels in motion,' came the steady reply.

'Is there anything else you require?' asked Amanda.

'No. Don't let me keep you from your other patients. They need you more than I do.'

Amanda gazed searchingly into the woman's face, but Margaret's features were expressionless, and Amanda departed, going back to her office. She asked Nurse Fleming if Doctor Ormond was around, and learned that he had gone to the first floor to see the patients there.

'Keep an eye on the office for a few moments, please,' said Amanda, 'just in case someone buzzes. I need to talk to the doctor.'

She found Richard on the first floor, and waited until he emerged from one of the rooms. He smiled at her, pausing at her side, and Amanda acquainted him with Margaret Sampson's wishes.

'I was half afraid of this,' he confessed. 'She is still trying to escape from reality. She'll do anything but face the psychiatrist. I think I'd better have a chat with her.'

'She's adamant in her determination to

leave,' said Amanda as they made their way to the stairs, and went on to describe her impressions of Margaret Sampson's attitude.

'That fits in with what I feel about her,' said Richard. 'Leave her to me, and I'll check with you after I've talked to her.'

Amanda went back to her office and sat down to face her paperwork, but her thoughts were with Richard, and when he entered the office some fifteen minutes later his face was set in harsh lines.

'I can't talk any sense into her,' he said heavily. 'Something has certainly upset her. Have you any idea what it might be?'

'I'd better tell you what she said to me first thing,' replied Amanda, and recounted her chat with the patient, explaining how Margaret had professed to be in love with Richard. He did not smile at her words, and his dark eyes narrowed.

'That does sometimes happen, but what concerns me is the change of attitude in her. She was not in the least concerned that we seemed to be interested in each other. In fact she talked about it when we were having tea together at the farm on that afternoon you first took her out. She seemed in favour of us getting together. But how did she learn of the progress our relationship has made?'

'I have my own ideas upon that,' said Amanda, 'but perhaps I'd better not voice them.'

'In view of the seriousness of this situation I think you should,' he responded gently.

Amanda nodded slowly. 'I haven't told you, but Nurse Brant seems to upset Mrs Sampson, and I've had to give orders that under no circumstances is she to attend Mrs Sampson. It was Nurse Brant who saw us together in the stable at the farm last evening, and Mrs Sampson said that Nurse Brant had been in to see her before I started my round. It's possible that she said something about us.'

'To one of the patients?' There was surprise in Richard's voice, and he shook his head slowly in disbelief.

'I'll have to go one step further and tell you that from the moment I met Nurse Brant there has been an intangible animosity in her attitude towards me.' Amanda spoke quietly. 'I don't want to make an issue of it, but there is something wrong. I put it down to jealousy. I believe she hoped to be promoted to Sister when the vacancy occurred.'

'You ought to have told me about this before,' he said, sighing. 'I'll talk to her, and if she did make any comment about us to Mrs Sampson then she'll be in hot water. But while I deal with this perhaps you'll telephone Mrs Sampson's parents. Acquaint them with their daughter's desire to discharge herself and get their reaction, although there's little they can do if she has made up her mind to leave. Arrange for them to come and pick her up, will you?'

Amanda nodded and sat down to use the telephone. She looked through Margaret Sampson's file and found her parents' telephone number, but when she called and spoke to Mrs Aston she discovered that the woman was completely dominated by her husband.

'I'm afraid I can't say anything. You'll have to talk to Mr Aston. I'll give you his number. Perhaps you'll call him at his office. But he'll be angry, I'm sure. You said Margaret was getting along very well.'

'Give me his number and I'll talk to him,' said Amanda, making a note as Mrs Aston rattled off a stream of figures. 'Thank you. I'll call him now.' She replaced the receiver, then lifted it again and dialled the new number. A moment later Mr Aston's harsh voice sounded in her ear. When Amanda gave him a report of the situation he exploded into a string of minor oaths, causing her to remove the receiver from her ear. When he calmed somewhat, Amanda spoke again. 'We cannot hold your daughter against her will or even on your orders,' she said. 'She is firm in her desire to leave us, so perhaps you would make arrangements to come and see her. If you want her home then she may return with you, but if you feel, as we do, that she ought to see the psychiatrist, then try and talk her into a different frame of mind.'

'I'll be there in about thirty minutes,' came the gruff reply, and then the line went dead.

Amanda wanted to get on with her work. The indicator board was buzzing, and several room numbers were illuminated. She stifled a sigh, for this was the way duty went. She walked to the door and peered into the corridor, spotting Nurse Fleming and calling to her. She went in answer to one of the calls and sent her subordinate to take care of the others.

Richard appeared along the corridor as Amanda emerged from a patient's room, and he came striding towards her, his face showing anger.

'I've had a chat with Nurse Brant,' he said firmly, 'and I have accepted her resignation.'

'Oh!' Amanda paused and gazed at him.

'Was that necessary? She's an extremely competent nurse.'

'In some ways she is, but discretion is an essential part of a nurse's make-up, and she admitted to me that she divulged certain facts to Mrs Sampson this morning. That accounts for our patient's change of attitude, and Nurse Brant's behaviour is inexcusable. She is resigning in order to save me having to dismiss her. She'll leave of her own accord and have good references.'

'I thought everything was going too well,' observed Amanda. 'Now it seems to be just the opposite.'

'Don't blame yourself,' he rebuked, meeting her gaze. 'You've done nothing wrong. Our personal lives have nothing to do with duty. But Nurse Brant is jealous of you, and we cannot work under such conditions. There must be no friction between members of the nursing staff.'

'But she was here before me,' protested Amanda. 'I feel guilty because she has to leave.'

'She's lacking in certain qualities, and because of those shortcomings she's unsuitable. Now I'd better get back to Mrs Sampson. Perhaps you'll bring her father along to her room when he arrives.'

'It might be better to see him on the side first,' suggested Amanda. 'He sounded angry over the phone, and he's certainly going to blame us for the change in attitude in his daughter. It might not be wise to let her overhear any altercation that takes place.'

'You think of everything.' He smiled and nodded. 'Keep him in the office and send for me when he arrives, please.'

Amanda nodded and went back to the office. Her head was aching slightly and a frown marred her smooth forehead. She was unhappy about the way events had turned against Thelma Brant, and wished there was something she could do to alleviate the situation. When she entered the office she found Thelma waiting there, a grim expression upon her face, and steeled herself for a scene, but Thelma merely asked a question about one of the patients, then turned to depart.

'Just a moment, Nurse,' said Amanda, sitting down behind the desk. 'I want you to know that I wish this situation hadn't arisen. I think you're far too good a nurse to be leaving like this.'

'I'm not concerned in the least,' came the immediate reply. 'I was getting tired of the place, anyway. I'll be leaving at the end of the month. From tomorrow I'll be on a different shift to you.'

'What went wrong? Why were you against me from the start? You said you didn't think you were ready for a Sister's job, so it can't be jealousy, as I thought.'

'That's right. It wasn't that. But now the axe has fallen upon my neck, so to speak, I might as well set you straight. I'm in love with Doctor Ormond. Despite the fact that he fell for you the moment he saw you I thought I might win him. But when he came after me this morning and told me I was through I realized that I didn't have a chance, so I resigned to save my reputation. I've got nothing against you, Sister. I hope you'll find happiness. I'm sorry that I did speak to Mrs Sampson about what I saw last evening in the stable, but she had mentioned to me that she felt attracted towards the doctor, and I had a foolish idea that I could use her as a lever against you. But it back-fired, and I've got what I deserved. I only hope I haven't upset Mrs Sampson too much. She was making progress with your help, and all I've done is succeeded in turning her against you.'

'Thank you for being honest.' Amanda sighed as the girl departed. She tried to get back to her paperwork, but heard the front doorbell ring. Moments later she heard Woody's voice in the corridor, and Mr Aston's harsh tones answering in brusque fashion. She arose as the porter paused in the doorway.

'Mr Aston, Sister,' he reported, grimacing as he stepped aside, and Aston came striding into the office.

'Where's the doctor?' he demanded. 'There's going to be hell to pay over this business.'

'Please lower your voice, Mr Aston,' retorted Amanda. 'We have sick people in here, remember. And we don't want to upset your daughter, do we? You haven't accepted yet that she is ill, and if you treat her as if she is normal then you could have quite a lot of grief on your hands. If you'll sit down here in the office I'll fetch Doctor Ormond.'

Her quiet, insistent tone seemed to have an effect upon Aston, for he grunted and sat down, then reached into his pocket for a packet of cigarettes. Amanda paused in the doorway and glanced at him.

'No smoking, please!' she said firmly. 'It's a strict rule in the Hall, as you know.'

He muttered something that was inaudible to her ears, and she smiled grimly as she went along the corridor to Mrs Sampson's room. This was one of those days, she reflected. Nothing was going right, and she would be relieved when the end of her shift arrived. But, more than that, she was concerned about Margaret Sampson, and wished that there was a solution to the woman's problems. There had to be one, she told herself, but they had not struck upon it, and that was the stumbling block.

TWELVE

Richard was with Mrs Sampson, standing by the window and talking steadily while the woman sat upon the foot of the bed and listened without apparently paying any heed to the words. Richard met Amanda's gaze and she nodded her head slightly. He came towards her as she held the door open for him.

'I'll be back to see you in a little while, Mrs Sampson,' he said. 'Sister Wright will stay with you until I return.'

'He's in the office,' said Amanda in an undertone as Richard passed her, and he thanked her and departed.

'So Nurse Brant is sacked!' observed Margaret, becoming animated with Richard's departure. 'She shouldn't be a nurse, and certainly not in a place like this.'

'The patient is always right,' said Amanda. 'You don't have to worry about her any more.'

'I don't have to worry about anyone. I'm as free as a bird. I'm leaving here as soon as my parents arrive for me. I've told Doctor Ormond that I'm leaving, and there's no way you'll be able to change my mind.'

'I have no intention of trying to,' responded Amanda. 'If you are set upon going home then I hope you'll find happiness, Margaret.'

'That's easy for you to say, having everything here that you want. But you deserve the best, and I hope you get it.'

'Thank you. But I'm certain there's happiness waiting for you, if you'd only go out and look for it.'

'I'd rather not discuss it, if you don't mind. My brain is reeling as it is. I've suffered a great deal in the past, and I have no intention of taking any more. I thought this place was a refuge for me, but it has changed, thanks to certain people. Now all I want is to get away and forget everything.'

'Do you want me to remain?' asked Amanda.

'If you would. I don't want to be alone when my father comes in.'

Amanda nodded, and moved to the window to gaze out at the view awaiting her eyes. She sensed that there was a great deal she could say to this woman, and yet was unable to find the right words. She felt inadequate for the first time in her life, and suppressed a sigh as she turned, for the sound of the door opening attracted her, and Richard appeared, accompanied by Mr Aston.

'We'll leave you talk to your father, Mrs

Sampson,' said Richard, glancing towards Amanda.

'I'd rather have Amanda here with me,' retorted the woman.

Mr Aston looked as if he would protest, but a glance at his daughter's harshly set face made him change his mind, and he shrugged and moved to a chair to sit down.

'I don't care who stays,' he said. 'You've been taking care of her, so you know just about everything there is to know about her. What's this nonsense about you not wanting to see that psychiatrist, Margaret? It's all been arranged. Go and see him this afternoon and then I'll come back this evening and talk to you. There's nothing I can say now except that you're a constant source of worry to your mother and I. We don't deserve this. You've had everything that money can buy. I think it's about time you showed some appreciation and behaved yourself. It's been some time since you parted from that good-for-nothing husband of yours, and why you continue to mope after him I'll never know.'

'You couldn't begin to understand how I feel, not in a hundred years!' Margaret glanced at Amanda, her face twisted with emotion. 'Do you see the kind of attitude I've had to tolerate? How do you make an insensitive man feel pity or sympathy? No wonder I've been dragged down so low.'

'If you'll excuse me,' interrupted Richard. 'I have other patients to attend to. But if you need to speak to me Sister Wright can summon me.'

He departed, leaving Amanda standing by the window, and Mr Aston glanced towards her.

'What do you think about this business, Sister?' he demanded. 'You're a skilled nurse. Do you think Margaret is fit to come home to us?'

'I'm in no position, and I'm certainly not qualified to pass an opinion,' replied Amanda. 'If Margaret saw the psychiatrist this afternoon we'd be more sure of our ground, but if she has no wish to pursue this matter to its logical conclusion then our hands are tied.'

'All right,' cut in Margaret, sighing heavily. 'I can see the way it is going to be. If I went home I wouldn't find any peace. My father would be nagging at me every moment we were together. That's how it was before. I don't think I want to go home, anyway. I just wanted to get away completely from the whole familiar scene and the same problems. I'll just stay here like a good girl, and see the psychiatrist this afternoon.'

Amanda suppressed a sigh of relief, and remained silent. Mr Aston glanced at her, then looked into his daughter's face.

'Are you sure?' he demanded. 'I promise you that if you do come home you won't be bothered. But you will have to snap out of this attitude that you have.'

'I'll stay here. I don't want to face the old business that existed before I came here. No wonder my nerves were shattered! I want some peace and quiet, and I'll get it here.'

'I don't know why the devil you have to

drag me from my work!' grumbled her father, getting to his feet. 'You're worse now than you were when you were three years old. I don't know what you've got to worry about. I'm the one with all the problems.' He walked purposefully towards the door. 'Keep me posted on the situation, Sister,' he said. 'I have to go.'

When he had departed Margaret looked at Amanda, smiling wryly.

'You see what I have to endure?' she demanded. 'I couldn't take any more of that. You'll get your way. I'll do as you want.'

'It's for your own good,' said Amanda. 'I'm sure you'll come to the right decision in the end.'

'Who's to know what is the right decision?' countered Margaret. 'I wish I were dead and out of this. Mrs Edmondson is lucky. All her worries are over.'

'You should count your blessings instead of dwelling upon your woes. Just think of some of the other patients in here! There are at least two who will probably be dead before the week-end is over.'

'We each have a cross to bear. Sometimes it is physical and sometimes it is mental, but it is there. Now leave me, please, Amanda. My head is throbbing. I want to try and get some rest. You want me well enough to go into town this afternoon, don't you?'

'Shall I close the curtains?' asked Amanda.

'Please. The sunlight is rather bright. I don't want to be disturbed until lunch.'

'Try and sleep,' advised Amanda, closing the curtains and then going to the bed as Margaret kicked off her slippers and lay down. She pulled a cover over the woman's body and smoothed it gently. 'I'll see that you're not disturbed.'

For a moment she stood gazing down at the woman, but Margaret had already closed her eyes, and Amanda departed, closing the door gently. She sighed heavily as she went back to the office, and firmed her lips when she heard Mr Aston's voice booming through the open doorway. Richard was in the office with the man, and they both looked at Amanda as she entered. When she explained the situation, Mr Aston arose from his seat.

'Thank God for that!' he said fervently. 'But I know my daughter, and I thought she'd come to her senses. All she wanted was some attention and sympathy. I think it's wrong to give into her. But I suppose you know your own job best. Let me know what that psychiatrist has to say, will you.'

'We'll keep you informed,' said Richard, getting to his feet. 'I'm sorry you had to be called in, but this was a crisis, and I fear you may be confronted with several more before your daughter is completely cured of her problems.'

Aston departed, and Richard sighed heavily as his brown eyes lifted to meet Amanda's gaze. She smiled at him and he nodded slowly.

'Thanks for the way you've handled this,' he said. 'It's been difficult, but I think you've got Mrs Sampson's measure. She's going to do everything you want, if you can maintain the balance in your relationship with her.'

'I hope there will be no more setbacks,' said Amanda. 'But she should be better after this first visit to the psychiatrist is behind her, don't you agree?'

'Yes. I think it is the biggest hurdle she'll ever have to overcome. After that it should be all plain sailing. If she's resting now we'll leave her until lunch. Then I'll see that you're relieved in plenty of time to take her into town. My father is going to drive you in, if I recall the arrangements correctly.'

Amanda nodded and he departed, leaving her to return to her paperwork. She sat down heavily, feeling as if she had been on duty for a week without a break, and in the back of her mind was the hope that there would be no other crises to trouble her.

At noon they began to serve lunch, and diets had to be scrupulously checked. Amanda was kept busy, ensuring that all the patients were fed and supervised, and before she really had time to consider, she had to go off duty and prepare to take Margaret Sampson into town. She went off to the staff dining room to have her own lunch, and was about to ascend the stairs to her room to change out of uniform when she decided to check that Margaret was getting ready for the trip. She went along the ground floor corridor to the woman's room and tapped at the door before entering. When she opened the door she found the room deserted, and the lunch tray was on the foot of the bed, the food untouched.

Amanda glanced at her watch, then went into the corridor, looking around for a nurse. Nurse Fleming appeared and Amanda called to her.

'Did you see that Mrs Sampson had her lunch, Nurse?' she asked.

'Yes, Sister. Is anything wrong?'

'She's not in her room and her food is untouched.'

'She said she was hungry when I took the tray in!' Puzzlement sounded in the nurse's voice.

'Have you seen her along the corridor since serving her?' persisted Amanda.

'No, Sister, but then you know what it's like at meal times. We scarcely get the chance to breathe.'

Amanda nodded and began a search of the ground floor, checking the rooms of the other patients, but there was no sign of Margaret Sampson anywhere. Sister Walters, who had come to relieve Amanda, emerged from her office and at once suggested that Doctor Ormond be informed.

'She went off once before, and was discovered walking towards the river,' said the Sister in a tone which sent shivers along Amanda's spine.

'Perhaps you'll call the doctor and tell him,' suggested Amanda. 'I'll continue looking around for her.'

'I'll get the nurses to check the other floors,' continued Sister Walters, hurrying into the office.

Amanda saw the Sister pick up the telephone, and hurried back to Margaret's room. The woman had not returned, and Amanda went into the clothes cupboard to check if any articles of clothing were missing. She found the woman's pink bedroom slippers on the floor of the cupboard, and a pair of walking shoes was missing. A dressing gown was hanging from a peg, and the blouse and skirt that Margaret had worn during their outings from the Hall were also missing.

Turning to the window, Amanda saw that it was opened slightly, and pushed it wide to peer out at the flower bed beneath. When she saw the unmistakable imprint of a woman's shoe in the soft earth she caught her breath, and turned swiftly as Richard came hurrying into the room.

'Have you discovered anything?' he asked crisply, and his expression hardened as Amanda explained. 'Look, I'll get a real search organized as quickly as possible. Perhaps you'll start looking towards the river, in case she has gone that way.' He paused when he saw the expression of fear which crossed Amanda's face. 'It may not be a serious attempt,' he added. 'She might be trying to teach us a lesson. But don't take any chances, Amanda. This could be very real.'

Amanda nodded and hurried from the room. She left the Hall and went around the footpaths between the flower beds, following them to the gate which led out of the grounds. When she had a clear view towards the river she peered around, but failed to spot Margaret's figure anywhere. Breathless, she almost ran along the path that led to the river.

The sun was bright, the air warm, and the breeze carried no relief in its breath. Amanda looked at the ground, half afraid of seeing footprints which might have been left by Margaret, but the path was hard-packed earth and no prints showed.

By the time she reached the riverside she was gasping for breath, and there was no sign of Margaret. Pausing to look around, Amanda saw a rowing boat on the river, and there was an old man in it, lounging on the stern seat, a fishing rod in his right hand. She ran forward until she was in earshot, then called loudly.

'Excuse me, but did you see a woman pass by here within the past thirty minutes?'

The man jerked up and looked around in surprise, his mouth gaping when he saw Amanda dressed in her uniform.

'Why, no, Sister!' he replied jerkily. 'I was taking a nap. I haven't seen anyone. Have you lost one of your patients?'

'One is missing!' Amanda turned when she heard the sound of pounding hooves, and saw Charles Ormond riding towards her from the farm. She gasped with relief and started towards him, and he quickly confronted her and dismounted.

'Richard called me from the Hall and explained,' he said sharply. 'Any signs of her?'

'No, and this man hasn't seen her.'

'She didn't seem to be the suicidal type,' said Charles Ormond.

'That's what I thought, but one can never be sure. Would you ride along the bank in one direction while I search in the other?'

'How long was she gone before she was missed?' he asked grimly.

'I don't know, but about thirty minutes, I would say.'

'Then if she had any intention of drowning herself she's had enough time in which to get it done.' His face was set in harsh lines and he shook his head as he swung into his saddle. 'I'll go that way,' he continued, pointing back along the way Amanda had come. 'I can travel faster on horseback, and she might have gone in the opposite direction if she decided that you might look for her at the nearest spot if she was suddenly missed.'

'Thank you. I'll continue in this direction.' Amanda began to walk on in the direction she had been following. Now the dread in her mind was beginning to take hold with grim certainty, and she had visions of the police dragging the river for a body. She began to blame herself for not keeping a closer observation upon the woman, but quickly realized that she needed to maintain a clear mind. Self-recrimination would not help in the least.

This was unfamiliar country to her, but she went on along the path beside the river, her gaze observant. There was a heavy silence that seemed oppressive in the heat of midday, and she felt uncomfortable in her uniform. When she looked around to scan the fields and ground she had already covered she saw a tall figure trying to catch up with her, and recognized Richard. She did not stop for fear that he had not discovered Mrs Sampson. Even seconds could be vital if the woman was somewhere along the bank and planning to commit suicide.

She watched the river as she walked, looking for items of clothing, or even sight of a floating body, and her heart thudded painfully in her breast as she let her mind wander back over the events of the morning.

Then she saw a woman's shoe lying on the path, with a broken heel, and recognized it as belonging to Margaret Sampson. She hurried forward and snatched it up, sighing heavily as she gazed at it. Hope and despair mingled in her breast, and when she continued her eyes were narrowed against the glare of the sun. Dare she hope that Margaret would not attempt suicide? If she was intent upon drowning then surely she would have plunged into the river at its nearest point instead of following the bank, unless she was trying to pluck up courage to take the decisive step.

There was a bend in the river, with a clump of trees growing in the narrow arc, and Amanda hurried towards them, almost certain Margaret would be there. She could see for a great distance beyond the trees, and the river bank was completely deserted. She was gasping for breath, and her legs ached intolerably. But she dared not stop, and when she tried to peer into the dark shadows under the trees Margaret's voice spoke to her, and at first Amanda could not pinpoint the woman's position.

'I thought you'd come after me if anyone did, and find the right direction.'

'Where are you?' demanded Amanda, looking around desperately. 'Margaret, please don't do anything foolish. Let's talk.'

'I'm up here, and if you come any closer I'll jump into the river.'

Amanda frowned as she stared into the shadows. Then she caught a glimpse of movement on a thick branch overhanging the river and saw Margaret seated upon it, some twenty feet out from the bank. There were no shoes upon her feet and her skirt was torn. It was difficult to see her face, and impossible to read her expression, but her tone had a hunted sound to it, and Amanda knew she had to proceed with caution.

'What on earth are you doing up there?' she asked. 'Please come down and let's talk about your problems.'

'Problems! That's all I keep hearing about. But I don't have any problems. All I have to do is slide off this branch and all my problems will be over.'

'That would be a tragic waste of life,' retorted Amanda. 'You're young, Margaret, and you could make a good life for yourself. Just think about it for a moment. You can end it all by going into the water, and your troubles will be at an end. But you're alive and healthy, and, if you die, by this time next week there will be nothing left of you. You'll either be buried or cremated, and that will be the end of Margaret Sampson. I don't think that's what you really want. Just consider it for a moment. No more sunshine. No more life! Let your mind recall some of the other patients at the Hall; those who are seriously ill. All of them would give almost anything for what you have right now – perfect physical health. So don't make a mistake and do something silly. Please consider, Margaret.'

Amanda had no real idea of what she was saying. She knew only the need to keep talking, for Richard was behind her and coming up fast. But Margaret had evidently let her mind slip out of focus.

'If you come any nearer,' she retorted as Amanda began to close in, 'I'll jump.'

'If you do it would be all over for you in a few moments, but what about your parents and the grief you would bring to them?'

'What do they care about me? My father hasn't an ounce of sympathy in him.'

'You said you didn't need sympathy, remember? And what about your mother? Are you prepared to leave her alone with your father and the misery of your death?'

While she spoke, Amanda moved in closer, although she knew she would have no chance of scaling the tree and getting to grips with Margaret, and even if she managed to reach the woman the perch was so precarious that she would be unable to hold her if she struggled.

'Why don't you shut up? For God's sake! Do you have to keep telling me that I have responsibilities towards others? What about those who had responsibilities towards me?'

They were ignored and I suffered. Why must it be me all the time who has to suffer?'

'You said yourself that everyone has to suffer in this life. Now please come down, Margaret, and let us talk this out. If I can't convince you that life is worth living then you won't have lost anything. There'll always be another time when you'll get the opportunity to end your life. If you really mean to do it then no one can possibly stop you.'

A shout sounded from along the path, and Amanda turned and saw Richard in the distance, running towards her.

'Who's that?' demanded Margaret. 'You've been keeping me talking while others are coming.'

Amanda was looking back along the path, and at that moment Margaret screamed, sending echoes through the heavy silence. The next instant there was a terrific splash, and Amanda swung round, gasping in shock as her wide gaze took in the disturbance of the river surface and the disappearance of

Margaret from her perch on the branch.

Without pausing to think, Amanda kicked off her shoes and ran to the water's edge, diving into the river, aiming herself for the spot where the water was disturbed. She took a deep breath and held it as she hit the water, and went down beneath the surface, her eyes open. But the greenish depths were murky and she could see nothing. She surfaced and gasped for air, then saw Margaret several yards away, head out of the water, arms thrashing wildly.

'I can't swim!' screamed Margaret, and disappeared beneath the surface again.

Amanda kicked out towards the woman. She was a strong swimmer and had won medals for life saving. She aimed herself for the spot where Margaret had disappeared and submerged. The next instant her outstretched hands touched the woman's body, and she grasped firmly and kicked back to the surface. When they broke out of the water Margaret began to claw at Amanda, filled with a blind panic, and her screams echoed across the river. Amanda was dragged under, and swallowed some water, but she forced herself back to the surface and broke Margaret's frenzied hold upon her, then dived and swam around the woman, coming up behind her and seizing her in an unbreakable hold, cupping one hand under the woman's chin. She began to strike out for the bank, taking Margaret with her, and now the woman had ceased to struggle.

It seemed like an age to Amanda, but in reality the whole incident was over in a matter of moments. She grasped at a half-submerged log that jutted out from the bank and began to haul Margaret across it. In the distance Richard's voice was still calling, and sounding closer. Amanda gritted her teeth, her strength almost spent, and concentrated upon holding Margaret, who seemed lifeless but suddenly came back to violent movement. Amanda gripped her and clung to the log for dear life.

'I'm not trying to get away from you!'

Margaret suddenly gasped. 'I can't swim! I'm terrified of the water. I didn't jump off that branch. I fell!'

'You fell!' Amanda almost swallowed a gallon of water. 'You idiot, Magaret!'

The woman suddenly began to laugh, and there was a note of hysteria in her tones. But Amanda let her continue, aware that it was a reaction to the situation, and she found herself laughing too. The next moment Richard appeared on the bank, stripping off his jacket, and he was about to plunge into the river when he spotted them beside the steep bank.

'Hold her, Amanda!' he called urgently. 'Don't let go of her whatever you do!' He paused then, for the sound of their combined laughter cut through the shock he was feeling. His expression changed, and Amanda laughed all the harder, for his face seemed so comical. 'What the devil!' he exclaimed. 'Are you both hysterical?'

'She didn't jump, she fell accidentally,' retorted Amanda, and Margaret laughed with mounting hysteria.

'Come on in, Doctor!' she called, her teeth chattering with shock. 'The water's lovely!'

Richard stared for a moment, then a smile broke out on his face. He clambered carefully down the bank and balanced on the log, bending to grasp Margaret, and Amanda pushed at the woman from behind. But Margaret reached out and clutched Richard's hand, then pulled with all her strength, toppling him off the log and into the water. Her laughter shrieked out as she began to drag herself out of the water.

Richard appeared yards away, and spluttered a little. His face was pale, but when he saw Margaret clambering out of the water unaided he smiled and came swimming to Amanda's side. Together they followed Margaret out of the water, and when they reached the grassy bank they collapsed together. Margaret was still laughing unrestrainedly, and Amanda was giggling.

'Are you all right, Mrs Sampson?' demanded Richard in worried tones.

'I've never felt better in my life,' came the giggling reply, 'and I'm not hysterical. You should have seen your face when you went over my head into the water. I fell in and got wet, so why shouldn't you?'

'The patient is always right,' said Amanda.

'This one is due to visit the psychiatrist this afternoon,' retorted Richard.

'That's one appointment you can forget,' said Margaret. 'I've finally come back to my senses, and I know I'll be all right now. You were quite right in what you said, Amanda, and I've been acting like a spoiled child instead of a responsible adult. I'm ready to go home now, and I'll be able to face up to my father and life in general. I have a lot to be thankful for, and most of all I'm thankful that you came to the Hall and took charge of me, Amanda.' She started to her feet, smiling, all hysteria gone, although her face was ashen. But her gaze was steady. 'I don't know about you two,' she continued, 'but I want to get out of these wet clothes, and I hope you haven't alerted the police, Doctor,

I don't need that kind of publicity.'

'I haven't,' said Richard, helping Amanda to her feet. He held her for a moment, while Margaret turned her back and started walking along the path towards the Hall. Then he leaned forward and gently kissed her on the lips. 'I have the feeling that, suddenly, all our problems have departed,' he commented.

Amanda made no reply. For a moment her mind was lost to duty and responsibility. She returned his kiss with a great deal of fervour, and as they turned to follow Margaret she knew that she had indeed found her niche in life. This was where she belonged, and the birds singing in the branches seemed to broadcast the fact as she and Richard walked hand in hand, soaked to the skin but very happy, along the path that led not only to the Hall but straight into a rosy future.

The publishers hope that this book has given you enjoyable reading. Large Print Books are especially designed to be as easy to see and hold as possible. If you wish a complete list of our books please ask at your local library or write directly to:

Dales Large Print Books
Magna House, Long Preston,
Skipton, North Yorkshire.
BD23 4ND

This Large Print Book for the partially sighted, who cannot read normal print, is published under the auspices of
THE ULVERSCROFT FOUNDATION